Neither Rebel Nor Tory

Hanyost Schuyler and The Siege of Fort Stanwix

by

Michael Cooney

Wilderness Hill Publishers
2007

ISBN 978-0-6151-7749-6

Wilderness Hill Books
75 Wilderness Lane
Valatie, NY 12184

wildernesshill@ gmail.com

COVER DESIGN: According to tradition, the
American flag was flown for the first time in battle
during the siege of Fort Stanwix in 1777. This is
one version of the original thirteen star flag that
may have flown above the fort.

Contents

Illustrations

*All illustrations and maps are from 18th and 19th century sources, with the exception of the photograph of Indian Castle Church.

Although this is a work of fiction, the people, places and events are closely based upon the historical record of the American Revolution in the Mohawk Valley of upper New York State. Hanyost Schuyler was a real person who played a critical role in breaking the British siege of Fort Stanwix in 1777. His appearance on both sides of that conflict is certain. Far less certain is who this young man truly was and how he was able to drive away an entire invading army.

1. The Boy Who Would Not Speak
July 1765

"Your boy has always been too quiet, Elizabeth, and now..." Nicholas Herkimer shook his head and paused to relight his pipe with an ember from the fireplace.

"He's like his father in that way, and then to lose him like this..."

"It does not seem natural, this silence of his."

"It's only his way, brother. His way of grieving."

"But finding his own Pa dead like that, and not saying a word?"

"He has only nine years, brother."

"Ah, nine is old enough to know your Pa is dead. And he don't weep nor say a word. Only look at his brother, young Nick. He has eleven years on him and yet he's able to talk about how fond he was of his Pa, isn't he? And to weep? And show that he is moved by the grievous loss?"

Just then, a commotion in the yard drew the landowner and his widowed sister to the doorway. Elizabeth, at 37, was a year older and slightly taller than her shorter and more compact brother. Her face was drawn and her eyes were red from weeping.

"Blast! Here come the redskins! Eager to get their share of the funeral meat and drink, I'll wager."

"Brother, be kind to them. You know what good friends Peter was with the Mohawks. A number of them were even at the church service, and behaved most solemnly."

"Oh, Liz, you have a kind word for everyone, though I could never see the where nor why of such friendships as your poor Peter kept with the savages. Even the ones that have gone off to Christian schools, like Joseph Brant there, still have black hearts."

Indian families continued to arrive in the spacious yard that stretched away from the brick manor house down toward the Mohawk River. They joined the white settlers who were already gathering around the long tables that Herkimer had ordered set up on the lawn. Black slaves, dressed in a uniform livery of light green, were hurrying out from the kitchen with great trays of food.

Young Brant, dressed in the fine English clothes that he had worn in school, saw Herkimer in the doorway and waved, motioning for him to join the milling crowd of Mohawks and settlers.

"Presently, my friend," called Herkimer. And then under his breath: "I must tend to our savage guests, sister."

"Joseph is not such a savage, brother," said Elizabeth. "Peter said that he is a born diplomat and speaks English better than you and I."

Nicholas looked sidelong at his sister. Like all the Palatine Germans of the Mohawk and Schoharie Valleys, the Herkimers were most comfortable in their native tongue, but needed English for business and legal dealings of all kinds.

"Linger a moment longer with me, Nicholas. Papa will make our guests feel welcome."

Their father, Johan Jost Herkimer, a huge man known to the Indians as Kouari, or Bear, was moving easily among the Mohawks and the white settlers. He was saying a few words to Joseph Brant before moving on to greet a grizzled old farmer in his native German.

"The Mohawks love Papa, don't they?"

"I don't know what's in their hearts, sister, but I do know that they respect his great strength."

"Peter said that they still tell the story of how Papa, on a bet, picked up and carried a dugout canoe weighing five hundred pounds."

"If anyone would know the tales of the Mohawks, it would be Peter," Herkimer half-laughed. "He spent many an hour at their fireside that would have been better…"

"Go, Nicholas, and see to our guests. I will join you in a moment."

Elizabeth stayed by the glass-paned window, watching Herkimer as he joined their father among a crowd of Indians. Her sons hovered near the men, young Nicholas closely following the conversation of his father and grandfather.

Hanyost, a small thin boy with flaxen hair, his head bowed, seemed unaware of his surroundings. He'll be well soon enough, she told herself. He just needs time.

Many of the Mohawks had worn their most European clothes to this occasion, the women in dresses made from red or blue trade cloth and the men in shirts and trousers of the same material. A few of the less prosperous still worn buckskin but even they had added some trinket or adornment purchased from the whites.

Elizabeth's mind was drifting back to a few days earlier. She was striving to remember the exact words that her husband had said to her as he went out to the fields on that last morning of his life.

Within a few moments, she heard steps behind her.

"Ah, Lizzie, no use in such melancholy thoughts."

Elizabeth Schuyler turned away from the fireplace and managed a faint smile. Her youngest brother Johan Herkimer threw a rough arm about her shoulders. "You've always been a strong girl, Liz. The Lord never gives us more'n' we can bear."

"How about yourself, Johan? And your debt to Sir William? How are you bearing that?"

"Ah, your husband's funeral day is not a time to trouble yourself about my affairs." Johan paused. He was a burly man, more resembling their father physically than either Nicholas or Elizabeth, but with a far less confident air. "But since you ask, I'll tell you. That rascally Englishman now owns my acres in Stone Arabia, plain and simple."

"But what will you do now? Will Nicholas…"

"My brother will be no help to me." Johan Jost Herkimer spat a gob of tobacco juice into the fire. "He's always been a hard man, like Papa. And he'll end up the richest landowner in the valley before long. As for me, I'm going to work for old Sir William Johnson himself. He's a clever dog, even more so than our dear brother, and may well give me a leg up in the world, now that's he's done cheating me." He laughed bitterly.

Elizabeth put her hand on her brother's arm, embarrassed for him as his eyes misted.

Johan coughed. "Enough about me. How is my little namesake Hanyost doing with all this sadness? He must be hard shaken."

"He is, Johan. He truly is. He has not spoken since finding his Papa dead in the cornfield."

"Not a word?"

"Not one. Nor eaten neither."

"Just sat there by the body, I hear. Is that how it was?"

"Yes, poor little Hanyost stayed by his Papa in the cornfield until finally I wondered what was keeping the two of them and I sent Nicholas out to make inquiry."

"Ah, Nick, my dear brother's namesake. And his very image, too."

"Nicholas came running back for me. As soon as I went and saw poor Peter, I knew he was with the Lord. His face had gone all blue."

"And Hanyost just sat there with his dead father for nigh onto two hours?"

"He did."

"I espied him at the burial service and the boy seemed like he hardly knew where he was. Like he was walking about in a dream. Do you think he fully understands what has happened?"

"He's not feebleminded," Elizabeth flared up. "If that's what you're thinking."

"I'm not saying…"

"He's just a quiet one, that's all. He's like his Papa in that way. There was many a time when Peter was so deep in thought on some matter or other that he wouldn't speak nor eat for days on end."

"Hanyost is like his Pa, then. You're saying that we needn't fret overmuch for him."

"Yes, though I confess I fear for him in a world as cruel as this."

"Ah, he'll be well enough. Better to be like his Pa than his Uncle Nick is what I say. Your man was always one who spoke his true mind without deceit, which is more than can be said for some!"

"Enough of such talk." Elizabeth took her brother's arm. "Let us go into the yard and help Papa and Nicholas welcome the Mohawk people.

They are our neighbors and were good friends to my Peter, God rest his soul."

Nicholas Herkimer's home, as depicted in *The Pictorial Field Book of the Revolution* by Benson J. Lossing 1859

2. The Boy Recovers His Voice

"Here comes Molly Brant, the sweet girl," said Elizabeth, stepping off the porch and walking toward the young Mohawk woman.

"That's exactly what Sir William says of her," muttered Johan but Elizabeth, if she heard him, did not acknowledge the comment.

As they embraced, Herkimer's sister began to weep, touched by Molly's sympathy. The Indian woman's glistening black braids and beadwork necklace contrasted with the new red gingham dress that she wore. The small girl by her side was clad entirely in buckskin.

Dabbing at her eyes, Elizabeth stepped back and bent down to embrace the girl, who was about the age of Hanyost, or a little younger.

"Ataentsic," she said, forgetting that the child only understood the Mohawk language. "Thank you for coming."

Johan left his sister in the company of the Indian women and made his way to a long table, which was being loaded down with food and drink by his brother's African slaves. "No beer, bucko?" he inquired of a young slave who was struggling to balance a tray of fresh baked trout.

"It's comin', sir," answered the young black man. "The beer is comin', sir."

"Forget the beer. I think you'll find this hard cider more to your taste," said George Klock, roughly pushing aside the slave and slamming a clay jug down onto the table. "I'll pour you a glass."

"Good strong cider," returned Johan, taking a gulp. "From your own apples?"

"Yep, mine and my brother's." Klock poured himself a glass. "But tell me, how is your sister holding up?"

"Well enough," replied Johan. "She's a strong woman."

"I see her there having a parley with Brant's sister Molly. I hear that Sir William fancies her." Klock nudged Johan. "I could fancy her myself, if I weren't the sound Reformed Church man that I am."

"Elizabeth's husband was friends with many of the savages." Johan was not eager to have his employer's new love interest maligned in his presence. "Not that it helped him in his business affairs with them."

"But aren't the Schuylers a wealthy family?"

"So my father thought." Johann drained his glass and Klock refilled it. "That's why he looked with such favor on Elizabeth's marriage to Peter even though he was a Dutchman."

"We can't all marry our cousins," laughed Klock. "Though it seems most of us do, don't we?"

Johann returned his laugh, looking over the crowd of closely related Herkimers, Bellingers, Timmermans and Snells, all descended from the first settlers who had come over with his father from the Rhine valley.

"Didn't your sister's husband buy a large tract of land from the Injuns over near Otsego Lake?"

"He and his father were partners in that venture, but the way I understand it, they never made a profit."

"How can that be? A white man always makes a profit when he trades with the Injuns. Give 'em a little rum and they'd sell you their grandmother."

"All I know is that Peter didn't leave my sister with very much."

"He died a poor man?"

"Elizabeth is very close-mouthed when it comes to anything that might put her husband in a bad light," said Johan. "But I fear that all she and her boys have is that small cabin over past the Mohawk village."

"I hold a deed to the land that village is built on," Klock confided. "All legal and proper."

"So I've heard," responded Johan with amusement. "And more than once."

"Of course, William Johnson wants to keep it for his brood of half breeds, so he's thwarted my claim at every turn."

"He and the Mohawks have always been fast friends, and that's the source of Johnson's power. And his power over the savages is why he's such a favorite of King George."

Johann liked Klock but could never understand why he was so openly hostile to the Englishmen under whose patronage the German settlers had come here forty years earlier and under whose rule they still lived. The English may have only wanted to settle us here as a buffer against the French, he reflected, but we've done well over the years.

"But Johnson is no true Christian!" Klock's face grew red with anger. "He's a heathen and joins in the pagan rituals of those damned Injuns."

"He's smart, that's what he is," Johann tried to explain. "I don't care if he does paint his face and dance half-naked around the fire with them. Without him and his Injun friends, we would've lost the war with the French and ended up bowing down to the Pope in Rome."

"The savages ought to go west with the rest of their kind, in my view, and leave all the good rich land to us Christians," Klock fumed. "We know how to properly make use of the Earth as God intended."

"Mark my words, George. The Mohawks will stay in this valley as long the English King wants them to be his allies."

"But why does the King need the damned savages now that the French are defeated and the whole continent is his?"

"I can't say, George," smiled Johan. "Maybe his great and powerful majesty needs all six of the Iroquois tribes to threaten us in case we forget to keep sending him taxes every year..."

"Very likely," Klock replied, his attention shifting to the other side of the yard. "It always boils down to money, don't it? But tell me, what tribe does that one over there belong to? The Ethiops?"

Johan looked where Klock had pointed, by the side of the smoke house. He saw that a tall dark-skinned Indian, wearing a huge bearskin cape, had stopped to talk with his nephew, young Hanyost Schuyler. The Indian was saying something very intently while Hanyost silently stared up at him.

"And isn't that your nephew, Schuyler's boy, that he's talking to?" asked Klock, squinting to get a better look. "That big Injun looks more African than redskin to me. Maybe he's one of your brother's new slaves."

"Nay, he's no black slave, tho he looks very like them," said Abel Hunt who joined the two men, pouring a glass of cider from the jug. "He has some long Injun name but folks call him Black Jacob.

They say he's a Tuscarora, one of the tribe that the settlers drove out of the Carolinas years ago."

"Aren't they the ones that settled out west near the Oneidas?" asked Klock.

"Yes, and that big black one should have stayed out there away from us white people!" Hunt was glaring at the man with a rage that Johan found hard to fathom.

"That old fellow seems harmless enough," said Johan mildly. "Boys always like Injuns."

"I wouldn't want him talking to a nephew of mine, that's all I'm saying."

"What kind of heathen mumbo-jumbo is that?" said Klock. "Look to him, Johan. He's wrappin' them beads round the lad's neck!"

The tall Indian held a string of white beads in both his large hands. He was moving them in front of Hanyost's eyes. Then he held the beads against the boy's neck, muttering in a low voice all the while.

Johan, alarmed now, moved quickly toward the Indian and reached out to pull him away from Hanyost. At that moment Joseph Brant stepped between the two of them.

"Hold, Mr. Herkimer. Jacob means the boy no harm."

"What?" Johan turned as if to strike the well-dressed young Mohawk, then stopped, unnerved by his steady gaze.

"The old one is helping the boy."

"What is he doing?"

"Among our people, when one grieves for a loved one who has gone to the Plentiful Country, the clear-minded come to bring them back to the daylight world. He wipes away the boy's tears so that he may see us again. He unplugs his ears so that he may hear us again."

"If you don't stop that savage from strangling the lad, I will!" exploded Klock, lunging toward the Tuscarora.

Brant reached out and held both of Klock's arms with a grip of iron. "Now he opens the boy's throat so that he will find his voice and speak to us again."

Klock twisted in Brant's grasp, unable to break free. Hunt backed away, afraid to interfere.

"Now he is done," said Brant, releasing Klock. "The boy will be well."

The young Mohawk spoke a few words to Hanyost and then led the old man away to join the other tribesmen.

The boy, his blue eyes wide, looked from one man to the other until he saw his uncle and smiled.

"I'm hungry," said Hanyost.

"You're talking again!" Johan knelt and grasped the boy in his arms. "Whatever that Injun did, he's got you talking again, thank the Lord!"

"I'm hungry," the boy repeated.

"Let's go find you something to eat, boy," said Johan, taking his nephew by the hand over to where his mother stood with Molly Brant.

Elizabeth reached out for her son and he began to run toward her.

3. Black Jacob
February 1768

On a bitter cold winter day three years later, the wind swirled down from the hills above the river and sent snow piling up against the sides of the tribe's four remaining longhouses and scattered log cabins. In each of the bark-covered structures of Connajoharry several families had traditionally lived, maintaining their own privacy while sharing in the rich communal lives of the people. Now, most families lived in separate cabins in the manner of their German and English speaking neighbors.

Winter had once been a time for telling of old legends and myths, for gathering around the firepit and doing the work of winter: transforming deer and bear skins into warm clothing and moccasins, shaping good strong bows and arrows, and chipping flint arrow and spear points. Now, during the short winter days the men of the village could more often be found at George Klock's tavern by the river's edge a half mile below the village.

In one of the longhouses, an old dark-skinned man and a twelve-year-old white boy were sitting beside a glowing fire. The man was finishing a tale of the first days of the world.

"And for this reason, the people could no longer understand each other's languages and there came to be many different tribes of men where once there had been only the single tribe of the people."

"But why is your skin darker than the skin of the other people of the tribe?" asked Hanyost.

"Now, show to me the arrowhead that you have made," said the old man, apparently ignoring the question. The boy selected one of the pointed pieces of flint that he had spread out on a piece of red cloth and handed it to the man.

Turning the flint in his large hands and examining it closely, the one whom the settlers called Black Jacob did not speak for several minutes.

"This work is good," he said finally. "You have chipped it well."

The old man settled himself down on the bearskin pallet, and took an ember from the fire with two sticks. His pipe was in the old manner, made of red clay, its bowl in the shape of Hadu, who wards off illness.

"Are you of the same people as those whom my uncle makes slaves of?" the boy persisted.

"I have named you He-Who-Listens," said the old man, allowing himself a faint smile, "but now I name you He-Who-is-a-Curious-Bird."

The air in the longhouse was already smoky from cooking fires as the old man exhaled clouds of blue smoke upward toward the vent hole. He picked up another flint arrowhead from the collection that the boy displayed. "This one is badly chipped. It cannot be fastened well with rawhide to the arrow shaft."

The Tuscarora sat, silently smoking. The boy remained seated at his side, unable to be as still as the old man, but trying.

A Mohawk boy, the same age as Hanyost, pushed aside the deerskin curtain and joined them. His eyes on Black Jacob, he too was silent as he sat down beside the white boy.

As the tobacco in his pipe burned down, the old man tapped out the ashes into the fire pit. Staring into the embers, he spoke.

"You two are of the age that I was when the wars came to my father's land. I had twelve summers when the peace between the Tuscarora and the English was broken."

The boys leaned forward, intent not to miss a word.

"I had learned from my father, as you have learned from me, how to chip arrowheads. First, finding the stone, then heating it. Then with a rounded piece of antler, beginning to bring the arrow-shape out of the stone. Slowly, slowly I learned to chip away the longer flakes from the stone. Like you, I destroyed many good pieces of flint before I knew how to chip away smaller and smaller flakes to make the sharp, killing blade."

The old man said nothing for a long time. Perhaps he was asleep? Hanyost turned slightly to see if the old man's eyes were closed, as they often were as he sat by the fire. But no, his eyes were open as he looked far into the past.

"My father taught me these things in the place that the English call Carolina."

"Your father?" Hanyost ventured, thinking of his own father, gone now these three years.

"In those days, all boys learned how to make arrowheads from flint. The settlers had not yet made steel arrowheads and hatchets to sell to us in return for our hunting lands. They did not sell to us their firewater or their weapons. They had their firesticks and steel swords and we had our flint tipped arrows and spears. My father had taken a vow never to use the white men's weapons. When I grew to be a man, I too made a vow never to use the metal weapons of the white men."

"Then there came a day when war began among the English. The white men split into two bands and fought each other for many days. Then one of the chief men of the whites, who was called Cary, came to the Tuscarora and offered muskets and whiskey if the people would attack the other whites, the ones who followed the man Hyde. Drinking the whiskey, many agreed with this foolish plan and attacked the other whites. Then the killing began."

"Did you fight in the war?" Hanyost burst out.

Onatah, the Mohawk boy, stared at him in embarrassment. One did not interrupt an elder as he told of the old days.

"My father did not want the war," the old man continued. "He did not want to go near the whites. He did not want their whiskey or their muskets."

"Was your father dark like you?" Hanyost interrupted again. This time Onatah jabbed his elbow sharply into his friend's side and hissed at him, "Be silent!"

Turning away from the fire, the old man looked at the two boys and smiled. Onatah was afraid. Mohawk men did not smile at boys like them unless they were about to play a joke.

"No, Curious Bird, my father was not of the dark skin. But my mother was. She was a slave of the whites in Charles Town. She ran into the forest to flee from their evil ways. My father found her nearly dead of hunger and took her to his village. He taught her to speak the true speech, as I have taught you, and he made her his wife. This is why my skin is as dark as the slaves your uncle keeps. They are my people too."

"So when war against the whites came, my father did not want to be part of the fighting. He knew that if the whites came and saw my mother, they would try to put chains on her and take her to their town. He knew they would see my skin and

23

put chains on me also. This is why he forbade me to join the other boys of the tribe on the path to war."

"Did not the mothers vote for war?" Now it was Onatah who could not restrain his curiosity,

"You are wise, young son of the Keepers of the Eastern Door of the Iroquois Longhouse," said the old man. "Among all peoples who speak the Iroquois tongues, only the mothers of the tribe may vote for war or peace and then the men must obey. But among the Tuscarora in those days, the war chiefs became full of pride, saying that they alone could decide on war or peace. When war came, many would go with those proud war chiefs but some would choose not to. My father chose not to fight for some whites against other whites."

Onatah's sister Ataentsic parted the deerskin curtain and sat beside the two boys.

The Mohawk boy frowned. Was this a storytime for girls or for men?

She raised her eyes questioningly to the old man, half-rising as if to leave.

"Stay, little one," he said, "if you wish to hear the tales of an old man."

"My father and mother stayed in our village," he resumed his narrative. "I was very unhappy not to go to war and I was angry at my father for this reason. But I could say no words of anger to him. Then fast-footed messengers came back to our village, saying that the whites had made peace among themselves and together they turned to attack our people. Many were killed and many villages burned."

"The Tuscarora chief whom the English called King Hancock called together many villages and said that all men of the nation must now fight the whites or all would die. Many of those who had not joined when the war was to help whites, now joined in the war against all the English."

"And then did you get to fight?" Hanyost burst out again.

"No, I did not," Black Jacob continued. "My father and mother came to me and we three went up into the high mountains where not even the Cherokee go. We stayed there for two summers until all fighting was done. All the villages of the Tuscarora were burned and many hundreds of the nation were dead. The few who were left came up into the mountains. My father welcomed them and it was decided to begin a long walk to the country of our brother people, the Iroquois."

"Was your father the chief of the people?" asked Onatah.

"He was not called the sachem, but it was he who walked in the first place when the Tuscarora people went north."

The old man was silent for a long time. "My mother was in the middle place with the women. And I was in the last place with what remained of the young warriors."

"We came to the country the English called Virginia," the old man spoke more rapidly now. The boys could hear his breathing become hoarse. "White men on horses were following us for three days. They were few and we did not attack them. We kept walking north. They came closer and then one of them seized my mother and threw her over his horse and galloped away."

"Why did they do that?" asked Hanyost.

"They were slave-catchers, hired by rich white men to find dark-skinned people who ran away from their big farms. They saw my mother's dark skin so they took her, thinking to get a reward from the white men for whom they caught slaves."

"I heard the shouts first, and then my father came running back through the forest. A group of young warriors joined us and we ran after the slave-catchers."

"They rode on horses and we only had our feet, but we ran by day and by night until after two nights we saw their campfire. We crept closer and waited for the moment to strike them. Then we saw that my mother was lying on the ground, not moving. The three white men were arguing with each other. Two dark-skinned men were chained to a tree."

"My father could understand the white men's language, and he told me that my mother had taken her life with the white man's knife. Those were the last words he said to me."

"Then my father ran to the white men and cut the throats of two of them with his flint knife before they could reach their weapons. I was right behind him and the other young warriors were with me. Then I heard the loud blast of the musket. The third white man killed my father. I cut the white man's throat and then I cut off his head."

The old man looked at the girl and the two boys. "But I would not kill the dark-skinned men. The other warriors wanted to kill them, too, but I found the keys to their chains and set them free. Then I buried my mother and my father in that place."

The Tuscarora stood up with difficulty, leaning on Hanyost. Beyond the bark-covered walls of the longhouse the wind grew stronger.

"Where is my stick?" he asked, a note of anxiety in his voice.

Ataentsic handed it to him and the old man went into his part of the dwelling, saying no more.

Iroquois women grinding corn or berries, by an unidentified engraver, 1664

4. White Boy
March, 1768

A few weeks later the cold grip of winter began to weaken and those of the people who still followed the old ways prepared for the Maple Syrup Festival. Streams, swollen by melting snow, rushed over the steep hillsides to the river and the first green sprouts of skunk cabbage and other early plants appeared.

Hanyost and Onatah had spent a fruitless day hunting for deer on the ridges above the Mohawk village. Each carried bows and a quiver of flint-tipped arrows, as they cautiously moved for hours through the forested hillsides. They saw only two deer, both too far away for an arrow shot.

"Why do you not bring your father's musket?" asked Onatah, as they stopped to rest on a hillside above the fast-flowing Nowadaga. "With the firestick, we could shoot farther."

"You know that I do not follow the ways of the white people. Like Black Jacob, I will use only the flint-tipped arrows that come to us from our mother the earth."

Hanyost looked out at the valley, where the fields and cabins of settlers had changed the land greatly even in the few years that he could remember. Patches of forest were smaller each year, and the faraway sound of the settlers' axes could be heard as the two boys sat and talked.

"The whites do not grow corn, squash and beans in the way that the Creator instructed us," Onatah said. "They cut down the trees and burn the stumps."

"They do this to make fields for their corn and wheat," Hanyost replied. "Then they feed most of the corn to their pigs. This is not right."

"But the true people plant the corn, beans and squash on the flat places along the river where the water is good and the trees do not wish to grow."

"This is true," said Hanyost. "I do not like the way that the white people take away the forest in order to make farms."

"Do you forget that you yourself are white-skinned?" laughed Onatah, holding his arm next to his friend's for comparison.

"Black Jacob does not have your color skin but he is one of the People of the Longhouse," Hanyost argued. "I am like him."

"But his father was a Tuscarora. It is true that he has the dark skin but he never lived with his mother's people."

"I choose to be with the true people." Hanyost's pale face was flushed with emotion. "I do not choose to be with the white-skinned people. I do not go to their school. I do not go to their church."

"But, my brother-friend, why do you so choose?"

Hanyost took some time to answer. "Do you agree that I speak your language?"

"Yes," conceded the Mohawk boy. "It may be that you speak almost as well as Sir William. All of the Iroquois people say that his soul is that of the Iroquois and that only his body is from the whites."

"So let them say of me." Hanyost was very serious. "But I will never buy the people's land as he has done."

"But why do you want this? Does it not grieve the heart of your mother?"

Hanyost paused to gather his thoughts. "I will ask you a question."

"Yes."

"Why is it that we see so few deer in the forests?"

Receiving no answer, Hanyost continued. "Our elder friend says this is because the white-skinned people have taken so much of the Mohawk land. They cut down the trees and make cornfields and cow pastures. They use their muskets to shoot even the mother deer and her young ones. Since this new treaty, the true people have no hunting ground left. They have only the two villages, Connajoharry and the lower castle that the whites call Fort Hunter. Soon the Mohawks will not even have those two villages!"

"So I have heard the old ones saying. They fear that when Sir William dies, there will be no other white chief to protect our land. Some of the warriors are angry even at Sir William and say that he has betrayed us in this new treaty. They talk of going away from the valley."

"They must not do this." Hanyost was adamant. "They must not let the white-skinned people take the whole valley! This is where the true people have come out of the earth and where the spirits of the old ones remain."

Onatah seemed not to hear him as he stared down at the fast-moving stream. "Look, my brother. Is not that our elder friend?"

"Black Jacob? Where?"

"There! He is wading across the stream of the Nowadaga."

"The waters are too fast," cried Hanyost in alarm. "He will stumble and be carried under the water!"

Suddenly filled with fear for their aged friend, the two boys scrambled down the hillside, grasping at roots to slow their descent, and plunging knee deep into the icy waters, just as the old man lost his footing on the slippery rocks.

"My brother, reach for his other arm," called Onatah, grabbing the old man as he fell forward. Struggling together, the boys managed to pull their friend out of the rapidly moving waters and onto the bank, where he collapsed on the wet leaves.

He struggled for breath, unable to speak.

"Grandfather," said Hanyost, using the Mohawk term of respect. "Why are you crossing the stream like this?"

"You young warriors have saved my life," the old man announced. "Now I must live long enough to repay the debt to you."

Then he smiled at the serious look on his rescuers' faces. "Come, help me up, young braves. My legs are frozen."

Leaning heavily on the two boys, the old man managed to walk slowly and unsteadily back toward the village.

"But why were you wading across the stream?" persisted Hanyost. "Where are you coming from?"

"I was visiting my dark-skinned brothers and sisters. I was learning some of the old ways of my mother's people from them, the old stories that they brought across the great water."

He breathed deeply for a few minutes before continuing. "I did not want your uncle's overseer to know I was there, so I came across the little stream."

"The stream was not so little, Grandfather," said Hanyost. "You might have been drowned."

The Tuscarora waved his hand dismissively, and concentrated on putting one foot in front of the other until the three reached the Mohawk village, where Onatah's mother welcomed him to her fire. She sent her daughter Ataentsic to fetch dry leggings and a deerskin tunic.

When the old man had warmed himself for a while, he spoke to the boys.

"You have saved my life, young warriors," he said, whether as a joke or in seriousness, they could not tell. "Now tell me how I may repay my debt to you two before my eyes close forever."

When neither boy spoke, the old Tuscarora looked at Hanyost. "Curious Bird, is there some question I can answer for you? Would that repay some of my debt?"

"Why do you want to know the stories and ways of my uncle's slaves?" Hanyost burst out. "I have heard my uncle say that they are not people but animals whom he can buy and sell."

"That is a good question." The old man accepted a bowl of corn soup from Onatah's mother.

"Since I owe to you my life, I will tell you an answer." He took a sip of the soup. "But first I will ask questions of you."

Hanyost nodded.

"Herkimer is your mother's brother, and yet you do not go to his big house nor sit by his fire."

Hanyost nodded again.

"You come to the fires of the true people. You sit beside this fire. You sit beside me, an old man whose people are not your people."

"Yes."

"And the son of this village," Black Jacob turned to Onatah, "has become your brother."

The old man reached for a stick to stir the fire, and continued. "Yet your mother's brother is a great man among your people. He has a big house made of brick, much cattle, and many fields of corn. Your own brother, the one called young Nicholas, goes to your uncle's house each day to join in his work."

Hanyost did not reply. His uncle's preference for his brother had been evident ever since their father died.

"Among the Iroquois," he continued, "a son looks to the brother of his mother as a second father. It is from his mother's brother that he gains knowledge of the daylight world."

Turning his head with difficulty, the old man looked directly at Hanyost. "Your brother works with the overseer of your uncle's slaves. What knowledge does your uncle want Nicholas to gain from this work?"

Hanyost was embarrassed by the question. He did not know what kind of work his older brother did at their uncle's farm. He only knew that Nicholas spent most days at the farm since their father died, and that his mother told him that their uncle's heart was sad because he had no children of his own. "He would treat you as a son also, if you would only let him," his mother had told him.

"Hah, white-boy-who-plays-at-being-Mohawk!" Hanyost felt a sharp jab in his ribs, and turned to see the leering face of Dadawat, an older Mohawk boy. "Can you not see that the black man is asleep?"

True enough, Jacob had dozed off, his chin dropping to his chest.

Onatah's eyes blazed, but he said nothing.

"Why do you sit with the white boy and the black man?" Dadawat taunted him. "Are you not a Mohawk?" Onatah still did not reply.

"Do you have no respect for the grandfather?" asked Hanyost.

"You think because you speak our language that you are of the true people but you are not!" spat Dadawat. "And your old black friend is not of the true people either! He should go live with his friends, the slaves of your uncle Herkimer. Let him be a slave of Herkimer too!"

When Hanyost said nothing, glaring at him in anger, Dadawat said, "Or do you not know that your old friend goes to visit the black slaves each day. Perhaps he has a woman among them? Or maybe you are his woman?"

Hanyost rose to his feet, afraid of the other boy but wanting to hit him.

"Oh, will you fight with me, white boy?" mocked Dadawat. "Wait, I will ask Onatah's little sister Ataentsic to battle for me. Then the match will be even."

Ataentsic, busy helping her mother weave a basket, looked up at her name. Hanyost's face reddened as he saw her looking at him.

Just then, the Tuscarora awoke with a cough, and Dadawat backed away, making an obscene gesture at Hanyost.

"I will go now, Grandfather," said Hanyost. He knew that Onatah could not speak back to an older boy like Dadawat, but his own fury at his taunts was great.

Once outside the longhouse, Hanyost looked for Dadawat, ready to challenge him but he had vanished.

Passing through a gap in the tilting and neglected palisades, Hanyost crossed the dry moat and left the village.

His mother's cabin was only a mile away, and Hanyost thought about his brother as he walked homeward. He wondered why his old Tuscarora friend had talked so much about Nicholas and the work he did at their uncle's farm, and what Black Jacob learned from talking with his uncle's slaves.

5. Festivals of Strawberry and Corn
June and July 1768

Although the winter did not return after that day, the cold never seemed to leave Black Jacob's body. He went no more to visit his friends among Herkimer's slaves. He slept by day almost as much as by night, and stayed close to the fire in the longhouse of Onatah's clan.

Ataentsic became his caregiver and Hanyost came nearly every day to the longhouse. At times she would let Hanyost help her in moving the old man or in feeding him spoonfuls of corn mush.

Onatah now spent more time with his mother's brother, who taught the boy how to use a musket. "In these days," he told Hanyost, "my uncle says that we must know how to use the white man's weapons. Of what use are the flint arrowheads that we made with the one whom the whites call Black Jacob? They will only shatter when war comes."

"When will war come?" Hanyost had asked. "And with whom?"

"My uncle says there will always be war. Only with the white man's firesticks were we able to defeat the Frenchmen and all the weak tribes that followed them."

Dismayed by his friend's new acceptance of ways that he disdained, Hanyost spent more time with Ataentsic.

"Do you remember how we played?" she asked one day.

"When we had three or four summers and my mother would bring me to the village?"

"Yes," she smiled. "I would make a little hut of branches and pretend that you were my husband."

Embarrassed by such childish talk, he said, "I do not remember these things."

"You promised to be my husband." She laughed and went back to helping her mother mash berries for the sweet drink of the Strawberry Festival. Unlike some of the older ceremonies, this was still an occasion when the entire village came together.

The broad meadows along the river were red with berries and all day the women and children had gathered the juicy fruit. Now women and girls prepared the drink which many of the men would mix with Klock's rum. Even so, the festival that year was a time of great joy and contentment in the village.

By midsummer, as the time of the Green Corn drew near, the old Tuscarora became even weaker. Whenever he spoke now, it was in a dialect that Hanyost, for all his knowledge of Mohawk, could not comprehend.

He and Ataentsic would sit on either side of the old man and as his words poured out, she would tell the boy what their friend was saying. Several times Joseph Brant came over from his new plank house at the edge of the village and knelt beside the old man and the two children. He found it hard to understand the Tuscarora's words and was eager for whatever Ataentsic could tell him.

"He talks much of the old days of his mother and his father who were killed," she said. "But other times he speaks of you, Hanyost, and of you, Thayendenegea, and of the wars that will be in the days to come."

"Does he know who we are to fight?" asked Brant. "Will the French come back? Will they make more trouble as they did with Pontiac and the western tribes?"

"He does not say. All he says is that he sees you leading many men and Hanyost is beside you."

There were other days when she did not translate any of what the one called Black Jacob said. "He speaks only to me now," she told Hanyost. "He tells me of the healing herbs of the forest, but I do not know all of the names he uses."

"Perhaps the old one knows that you will be a healer," said her mother, who had joined them. "When your children are born and grow to be men and women, there may come a time when you will be a wise old woman, my daughter. Perhaps this is what the our Tuscarora friend sees."

As the people of the village made ready to celebrate the Green Corn Ceremony, the old man died. Hanyost had been away with his mother and brother, visiting her father in German Flatts. By the time Hanyost returned, the people had celebrated their thanksgiving for the ripening of the corn and the old one had been buried in the ancient way on a hillside above the valley, facing the morning sun.

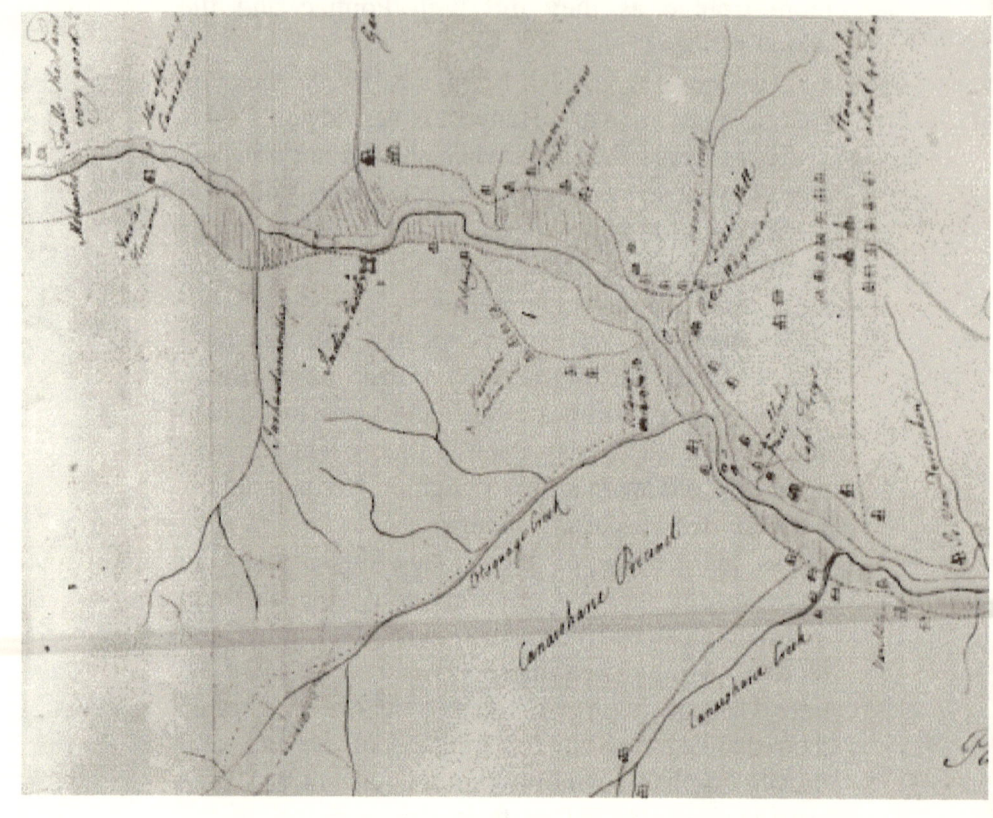

From the collection of the New York State Museum

1757 British map showing Connajoharry (Indian Castle) on the Mohawk River opposite the mouth of East Canada Creek, between present-day Little Falls and Fort Plain, NY. Hanyost's home would have been in this vicinity.

6. To Be a Grown Man
October 1771

Three winters passed and another could be felt in the cold west wind. The leaves had turned golden and red, and smoke curled up from the longhouses and cabins of Connajoharry. Hanyost stood on the low hill where his family's single cow grazed on the last dry grass of summer and looked toward the village.

Surrounded by a palisade wall and sharpened stakes, the village had been built as a fortress against attacks by the French and their Algonquin allies, but in the years of peace since 1758, the old defenses had fallen nearly to ruin. The dry moat was now filled by debris.

Cabins, hastily assembled from logs and planks scavenged from an old British fort, had grown up outside the walled village, stretching west along the flood plain toward Nowadaga Creek.

Hanyost came down the hillside toward the village, eager to find his brother-friend, Onatah. A day earlier, for the first time in months, they had seen deer on the ridge above the village. Now, they planned to return and hide in the tree branches to wait for the white-tails to pass by.

Hanyost and Onatah had each counted fifteen summers, and were both of an age to be men in the eyes of the tribe. However, Hanyost, despite his growing skill with the bow, had not yet killed a deer. The Mohawks, no less than the settlers, had come to rely on flintlock muskets for the hunt, and both regarded Hanyost's reliance on the more archaic weapon to be an eccentricity.

Despite his great desire to be a true son of the Mohawks, the men of the tribe did not invite him to join in their extended hunting journeys into the mountains where deer and bear were still plentiful. Onatah, he reminded himself, had killed a deer and he had not. But he used his uncle's musket, Hanyost told himself. I must use my bow in the old way.

Hanyost longed for a glimpse of his friend's sister, Ataentsic, who lately seemed to have become elusive. When they both were small, he would sit with her for hours as she played, pretending to cook for him. Unlike the Mohawk boys, he saw no shame in playing imaginary games with a girl. Then when Black Jacob was dying they had become close again.

In the summer months he had sought any opportunity to cross her path, though they had been few. Now, he felt a sudden burst of joy as he saw her emerge from the family longhouse, her long black hair carefully braided.

"I wish to you good morning, little sister," Hanyost spoke rapidly in Mohawk. Her arms were full of bearskins that she was shaking out in the morning light. With a stick she beat the dust and stray insects from the skins. She looked up at his approach.

"I perceive that my brother goes to hunt the white-tail deer." Ataentsic's words were formal but her smile was warm. "May she leap in front of your arrows, older brother."

"I will bring to you a deerskin," offered Hanyost, imagining himself presenting the fresh skin to her. Unlike most of the young women of the village, she did not care for cloth garments. "So that you may make a new dress for the Midwinter Festival."

"This winter will be cold, older brother. The summer birds have already flown away. Will my older brother not bring me a bearskin so that I may be warm on the cold nights that are coming?"

"One day I will bring you a bearskin large enough to make two people warm," Hanyost said.

Ataentsic looked up quickly at his bold suggestion. She called him "older brother," but always with a smile, and never with the looking-down-glance that accompanied her use of the same term with Onatah. He blushed, afraid that he had offended her, and at that moment his friend Onatah came out of the longhouse, stretching and yawning.

"Lazy fox!" called Hanyost, relieved by the distraction. "How will you catch the rabbit?"

"Today, little brother, I will bring home the deer. Rabbits are for small dogs like you."

The boys began to scuffle playfully, their usual greeting, as Ataentsic returned the bearskins to the family's sleeping pallets. As the boys left the village and ascended the hillside, Hanyost looked back toward the fields where his friend's sister had joined the other women in gathering pumpkins from among the dry corn stalks. She seemed to look up, her eyes searching for him, but he could not be sure.

That evening as the sun went behind the mountains and the air grew cold, the boys came down the wooded slopes and out into the open fields. They passed the new missionary church, erected a year earlier, and came back into the village.

Their game bags were full with rabbits, turkeys and wood grouse, good food for their people but not the prize that would assure Hanyost the status of a grown man.

As Hanyost and Onatah entered the longhouse, they passed through the quarters of other relatives before reaching the section where Onatah's mother was repairing a frayed basket. "My brother-by-another-mother and I bring you meat," announced Onatah, placing the game before her.

Onatah's mother greeted the two young men with the looking-away glance and uttered the ritual prayer for living beings who become food for humans. "The mother of your brother also has sons who hunger," she said. She picked the fattest turkey and rabbits and pushed them toward Hanyost. With respect, Hanyost pushed back her choices, until she again pushed the game to him, and he placed the meat in his deerskin pouch.

Hanyost heard giggling from behind the painted deerskin curtain-wall. Ataentsic?

Another giggle. He looked at Onatah in puzzlement. His Mohawk brother whispered. "My sister plays grown-woman games now."

Puzzled, Hanyost turned to leave, remembering that he had promised to be home before full dark. "Mother-of-my-brother," he said to Onatah's mother, "May good spirits only be inside the walls of your longhouse."

Another giggle, and this time he heard a male voice. The deerskin curtain flapped aside and Hanyost saw the older Mohawk boy whom he had detested for so long, Dadawat.

Without thinking, Hanyost began to move toward him, his hands curling into fists. Onatah stepped in front of his friend, pushing him out of the longhouse.

7. Sister of His Brother

"Why is Dadawat with your sister?" Hanyost asked, anger in his voice.

"They are playing grown-man grown-woman games," Onatah explained. "Now go. Take the meat to the house of your mother."

Hanyost's knowledge of the Mohawk ways of courtship was incomplete. "But your mother.... does your mother know this? Does your mother permit the...games?"

Onatah was puzzled. "My sister is of an age for grown-woman games and Dadawat wishes to be her hunter."

Hanyost's Mohawk was good, but he had not realized that the word for hunter had other meanings, as well. "Ihr Ehemann?" he asked in German, then in English, "Her husband?"

"Dadawat is from the Bear Clan. It is arranged by the mothers of the tribe that he will come to live at our hearth and be the hunter for my sister and mother, just as it is arranged that I will become the hunter for the sister of our hunting brother Tehorakwaneken of the Wolf Clan."

Hanyost began to understand. "Among your people, do the mothers tell you whom to marry?"

"Satahon'satat!" said Onatah. "Listen! My brother, there is much you do not know of our customs." Onatah led Hanyost onward, through the tilted palisade wall toward his family's cabin.

"I will explain as we walk together. The mothers keep the old laws of our clans, and the laws say that a hunter may never go to live at the hearth of a woman from his own clan. The mothers tell their

45

daughters that they may choose only from among men of the other clans."

"Your sister can choose one of the men from the other clan?" Hanyost was beginning to understand, "and she chose Dadawat?"

"It is like this," Onatah explained. "My sister and Dadawat see each other and give glances. Our sister tells my mother of the glances. My mother tells the mother of Dadawat that he may come to our hearth. They play the grown-man grown-woman games and laugh together. If they laugh much and have joy in each other, then the mothers talk again. Sometimes the two do not play the games well together, and then the woman will glance at another man from a suitable clan."

"I understand," said Hanyost. "But I..."

"But they must not do more than the games." Onatah spoke. "They must not make a baby together until the mothers talk again, and the hunter is welcomed to the hearth by the mother of the woman. Then he becomes her son and hunter."

Hanyost felt a flare of jealousy in his heart. Had he not exchanged glances with Ataentsic, and only this morning? Would he not be happy to come and live at her mother's hearth? Why did she not ask her mother to let him come and play these games?

"Then, Ataentsic ...our sister," he fumbled for words, "will marry Dadawat?"

"When the corn ripens again, my brother."

Hanyost was saddened that Ataentsic was beyond his reach, but he told himself that he could not question the old ways, handed down by the mothers. I am a brother-friend to Onatah, he reasoned, touching the turtle shell amulet his friend had given him. I am one of the Turtle Clan. My brother's sister cannot be for me.

The white boy clasped his friend's hand, and returned to own family's cabin, struggling to convince himself that he did not care as deeply as he truly did for the Mohawk girl.

8. The Coldest Winter
January 1772

The winter that came down on the valley soon after this day was a long and hard one. By late November the doorway and windows of the Schuyler cabin were blocked by deep and hard-packed snow. Hanyost broke a hole through the roof of the cabin, so that he and his mother could go in and out. He made new snowshoes in the Indian manner, of supple branches and rawhide, in order to cross swiftly over the deep snowdrifts.

"Johan Jost," his mother said to him one dark evening when he returned from an unsuccessful hunt, "I know that you do not wish to take anything from your Uncle Nicholas."

"What is it that my uncle wishes to give?" returned Hanyost.

Elizabeth set down her knitting. "He sent his overseer here while you were out. The man brought word of your brother."

"He is not sick?" Hanyost's heart leaped with alarm. Despite their growing sense of distance, he cared deeply for his brother. He knew that sickness filled the closed smoky rooms of the whites in the cold season.

"Your brother is well. The overseer says that your uncle has put him in charge of the slaves who do skilled work in the winter, repairing leather harnesses and broken farm tools."

"I am glad of it."

"And your uncle makes an offer for us to go also and live at his farmstead." Seeing an angry look cross over her son's face, Elizabeth hastened to add. "Only for the winter months. My brother says that I can help with the kitchen work and you can help in Nicholas' work."

"My uncle will allow us to be his slaves?"

His mother was surprised at the bitterness in her son's voice.

"Not slaves, son. Family. He will have us stay with him as family."

"You can go if you wish. I will remain here."

Elizabeth looked intently at her younger son. "Why do you have such anger at your uncle?"

"His ways are not my ways, my mother," Hanyost tried to explain. "When he speaks to the People of the Flint, he does not use the voice for speaking to the People of the Flint."

"I do not understand." Elizabeth was troubled. "Who are the People of the Flint?"

"They are the people you know as the Mohawks." Hanyost struggled to translate ideas that were only present for him in the Mohawk language. "It is like this. When people speak to those of their own tribe, they speak in one way."

"Yes?"

"And when they speak to enemies, they speak with another voice. I have heard my uncle use the voice of speaking-with-enemies when he speaks to Mohawks. And he uses that voice always when he speaks with his slaves."

"Hanyost, you spend so much time with your Mohawk friends that sometimes I do not know what you are saying."

"I will not listen when my uncle speaks with that voice to you," Hanyost concluded. "And this is why I will not sleep in his house."

Elizabeth reached forward to touch her son's hand. "I think I understand you, Johan Jost. I will remain here with you."

As that winter wore on relentlessly, the small family subsisted on dried meat and corn meal, and for drinking water they melted snow. Hanyost chopped holes into the frozen river and fished through the ice to supplement their meager diet. Far from other settlers, the mother and son managed to avoid the coughing sickness and the flux that carried away many, Iroquois as well as whites, that winter.

Although the cold moons were a time for winter games among the Mohawks, Hanyost avoided the village this year, pleading the need to provide fish for his mother. He made fresh bows and arrows from saplings he had cut in the Fall, and tipped the arrows with the feathers of high-flying birds.

Out on his snowshoes, he would wave to Mohawk friends and sometimes come close enough to talk, but Hanyost did not want to see Ataentsic and the boy with whom she was playing the grown-woman games. Despite his resolve to accept the ways of the clan, he kept turning over in his mind stories of Iroquois women marrying whites.

The Christmans and the Timmermans both had Indian women in their families, and he knew that Sir William Johnson, the King's agent for the valley, had married Molly Brant in a tribal ceremony and had children by her.

The Mohawks will accept white husbands for their daughters, Hanyost reasoned, as he worked out conversations in his mind about how he would speak to Ataentsic and with her mother. Or should he begin by speaking with her mother's brother? He wanted to ask Onatah but he sensed that speaking about such a matter to the brother of the young woman was never done. He longed to share his thoughts with his old friend but the Tuscarora was dead now for three winters.

Unsure with whom he could share his thoughts, and knowing that he must not talk with Ataentsic or her brother, he put off taking any action at all as the winter deepened and grew, if possible, even colder.

9. The Flight of Onatah
February 1772

One very cold morning in late February, Hanyost was alone on the frozen river near the mouth of Gaioharo Creek, trying to break a hole into the rock-hard ice so that he could drop a fishing line. The Mohawks thought it foolish to use a hook and line, preferring nets or a spear, but Hanyost had learned from his father to fish in this way, even in midwinter.

Wind-driven snow limited his visibility and Hanyost felt as if he were the only human in the snowy world. He tried to remember the story of the world's creation, when the Great Spirit brought the first summer and drove away darkness and cold. Or perhaps it was God the Father who did that?

Then he saw a figure moving uncertainly across the ice. He called out in a friendly way and was surprised when it was Onatah's voice that replied, "My brother!"

Hanyost stood up and waved, but when his Mohawk friend drew close, he was shocked to see that Onatah wore no snowshoes and was trudging through knee-deep drifts in only his thin summer deerskins and moccasins. Such garments would soon mean death in this weather.

His friend's face was contorted with unusual emotion. "My brother," cried Hanyost. "What has happened?"

"I walked away from my village." Onatah was out of breath and shivering uncontrollably. "I have taken life."

"What life? Who?"

"Dadawat has disgraced my sister. He has made a baby in her belly. Then he laughed at her and told her that he would never come to our hearth to be a hunter for my mother."

"How can that be?" Hanyost pulled off his woolen cloak and wrapped it around his friend.

"Dadawat mocked my sister. He said that he was promised to the hearth of a girl in the lower castle at Tionderoge. I went to his longhouse and told him he was a dog. He struck at me with his tomahawk, but he is weak and foolish. I took his own tomahawk and split his head. He fell dead. Now I must go away from my village."

"You will die in the snow, my brother." Hanyost thought quickly. "Come to my mother's cabin. You can stay with us."

"I cannot stay at your mother's hearth. The family of the one I have slain will seek to take my life." Onatah's entire body was shaking from the cold. "It is better if I die in the snow. Then the blood shedding will end with me."

"But you can go to Johnstown to appeal to Sir William," pleaded Hanyost. "You can explain to him that you did this deed in self-defense."

"My friend," said the Mohawk boy. "Sir William does not make law for the people of the Six Nations. When one of our people takes life, there is no prison and no hanging and no self-defense. The family of the one who is slain must spill the blood of the killer."

"But just come with me. You will soon freeze to death here."

"If I die here in the snow, then my family will not have to seek revenge against the family of the ones who must take my life. My death will bring peace to the families. This is why I choose to die here." Onatah sat down on the snow and began to chant.

Hanyost pulled the Mohawk boy to his feet and struggled to keep him upright. Onatah flailed out at him but the cold had already made him too weak to put up much resistance to Hanyost's efforts.

"I am bringing you to our cabin," Hanyost insisted. "We have warm robes and a good fire."

By now, Onatah seemed to be drifting off to sleep and Hanyost knew that was a sign that death was near. Slinging the other boy over his shoulder with great difficulty, Hanyost slogged through the rising blizzard away from the river. The extra weight made his snowshoes sink deeply into the snow. He found it harder and harder to take each step forward.

Finally, Hanyost could see the eaves of his mother's cabin, the only part visible above the huge snowdrifts.

Clambering up onto the roof, he carefully lowered Onatah down into the Schuyler cabin.

"Quick, mother," he called out. "I found Onatah on the river. He is freezing!"

Elizabeth Schuyler took the unconscious Mohawk boy and wrapped him in a quilt, chafing his hands and feet to restore circulation.

"I think he has escaped frostbite," she said to her son, as color returned to the boy's fingers and toes.

"But why is he outside in this summer garb?" she asked, puzzled.

Hanyost then explained his friend's plight.

"We must help him," his mother said simply. "You did right in bringing him here. He must go far away, and he will need sustenance for the journey."

Going to her pantry, Elizabeth found cornbread and some smoked beef. She picked out warm woolens and the thick deerskin boots of her husband and handed them to Hanyost.

"Let your friend rest now," she told her son. "The young ones recover quickly from what would kill someone my age."

Onatah slept for many hours, and awoke just before darkness fell. Looking around in a moment of panic, he made as if to bolt from the cabin, then saw Hanyost and his mother.

"Thank you," he said in English, as Elizabeth handed him a piece of cornbread from a newly baked loaf.

"You are most welcome," she replied in her thickly-accented English.

"You will not let me die," Onatah said in Mohawk.

Hanyost translated his friend's words for his mother.

"No, we will not." Elizabeth Schuyler was firm.

"I cannot stay with you. I will bring danger for you when the family of the one I slew comes for revenge." Again, Hanyost translated for his mother.

"Then you must go far away," said Elizabeth. "I have prepared food and warm clothing for your journey."

"Where will I go?" Onatah asked.

"I am thinking of the words of our grandfather-friend," said Hanyost in Mohawk. "I am thinking of the land of his people, the Tuscaroras, the younger brothers of the Oneida."

Onatah's spirits seemed to revive at this suggestion. "This is a good thought. I have heard that the Oneidas and the Tuscaroras adopt people from many tribes into their own, for disease has made their numbers grow small."

"There are few whites in that country and the hunting is good," continued Hanyost.

"You have spoken well," said Onatah. "I will go to the lodges of the Tuscaroras."

"I will walk with you on your journey and then return to this cabin."

Elizabeth's eyes darted back and forth between her son and his friend, picking up a word or two of Mohawk here and there. As the conversation ended, Hanyost explained to his mother that he planned to accompany his friend to the edge of Oneida country.

"It is something that your father would have done," said Elizabeth. She then gave each of the boys pouches heavy with food. They pulled on the warmest clothes, both woolen and deerskin.

When it was fully dark, the boys climbed back out onto the roof of the small cabin, and looked eastward. The snow was falling again and Connajoharry, a mile or so away, could not be seen.

"We must stay off the hunting trails of the Iroquois and the roads of the white men. If we walk on the frozen river toward the setting sun, we will come to the land of the Oneidas."

"Let us go," said Hanyost.

Before stepping out onto the snow, the two friends put on their snowshoes and were soon walking westward on the solid ice of the river.

Behind them, the falling snow quickly hid their tracks.

In the darkness they could barely see the outline of the grist mill at Little Falls, and at daybreak they passed the small village of German Flatts on the banks of the river. Smoke curled up from the cabins, and Hanyost could see the tower of the stone church and beside it, the place of upright stones and wooden crosses where his father's bones had rested all these years.

Although Hanyost was seldom inside a church, his mother had told him about Jesus and how he cured the sick and walked on water. "Jesus, help us in our journey and keep the evil winter spirits far away," Hanyost muttered under his breath.

They spent the next three nights in deep woods, burrowed into the snow, sleeping close together for warmth. On the fourth morning, the two boys were near Oneida country, a land into which neither had ever gone. And beyond that lay the villages of the Tuscaroras.

"You must leave me here," said Onatah. "I do not know if the Oneidas and Tuscaroras will understand that you are my true brother."

"Are you certain that they will let you sit at their hearths?"

"No one can be certain in these times when the white men change so many things, but it is the old law that no Iroquois-speaker will turn away another Iroquois-speaker, ever since the covenant of the Five Nations was given to us by the Lawgiver."

The snow had ended and the day was bright and clear. In the distance the sun glinted off the icy expanse of Oneida Lake. Hanyost saw sorrow in his friend's face.

"When will you return to Connajoharry?" asked Hanyost.

"I do not know. The mothers of the tribe will decide if, after a time, the grave of the one I slew can be covered."

"Covered?"

"This means that my family will give gifts to the family of the one I slew. If they are pleased with the gifts, the family can agree that the grave will be covered."

"That means that they will not seek revenge?"

"Yes, but only if they so choose." Onatah looked toward the unknown country to the west. "But in the old legends those who took life were banished forever."

Hanyost turned his face and spoke with the looking-away glance. "I will hunt in this country in the Spring. We will meet then, my brother."

"We will meet in the Spring," agreed Onatah, tightening the rawhide straps of his snowshoes.

Then he said what Hanyost knew was a hard saying for him. "When you hunt, bring meat to my mother and sister. My mother's clan is small and many hunters have died of disease."

"I will," promised Hanyost.

"O'nen," Onatah said. "Goodbye."

Hanyost nodded, and his friend vanished into the thick woods that surrounded the lake. Feeling suddenly very alone, he cried out to the Great Spirit to go with his friend, and began his own long trek homeward through the snow and ice.

Twentieth century view of Indian Castle Church
(Sir William Johnson's Anglican chapel at Connajoharry)

10. Sir William's Church
April 1772

In the following months Hanyost gained skill as an archer. In late winter, he finally killed his first deer.

He taught himself how to dress the meat and learned slowly how to prepare the skin for use as clothing. His mother helped him, using the skills she had gained as a girl working with slaughtered cattle on her father's farm.

With great pride he brought a gift of deermeat to Onatah's mother. At first his friend's mother pushed back the gift, but the food gathered in the previous summer was growing low and the coughing disease was taking many lives in the village. She accepted the gifts, and gave him in return a fine beadwork bracelet for his mother.

One afternoon in early Spring, as Hanyost was passing the white-painted church built by Sir William just outside Connajoharry, he was startled to see what he took to be a ghost.

"Dadawat!" he exclaimed before he could stop himself.

The young Mohawk whom he thought Onatah had killed was standing at the entrance of the church. Not sure if he faced a spirit or a living enemy, Hanyost saw a jagged white scar extending from Dadawat's hairline to his jaw.

"I thought you were..."

"You thought I was dead," said the Mohawk, "but through the grace of Jesus I was brought back to life."

The minister, a lean man in a black frock coat, appeared in the doorway of the church. He rested his hand on Dadawat's shoulder.

"Welcome, my son."

Seeing Hanyost, the minister beckoned to him. "Come, you too, my son, and enter the house of the Lord. Take instruction here beside your tawny brother so that you also may come to the table of the Lord."

"Much thanks, sir," murmured Hanyost, backing off. "I must be about..."

"We must all be about our Father's business, my son," said the minister, searching his face. "I cannot recall seeing you at divine service."

"Much thanks, sir," repeated Hanyost, turning away.

Two weeks later, Hanyost had occasion to see one of the leading Mohawks, Tekarihoga, about some tools that the sachem wanted to have repaired by the blacksmith in German Flatts. He asked Hanyost to negotiate a fair price for him, and he readily agreed.

After further courteous circumlocution, Hanyost mentioned the church just outside the village.

"That is the church that Sir William loves," observed Tekarihoga. "He was most gratified that Thayendenegea, whom you know as Joseph Brant, gave him land for the building of this church."

"Sir William is well pleased with Thayendenegea."

"And the Mohawks are pleased with Sir William."

"I was passing Sir William's church and I saw the one whom my Mohawk brother struck with a tomahawk. Does he go often to that church?"

"It is true that the one of whom you speak did go to that church." Tekarihoga made a sound of disgust. "But the clan mothers did not want him in Connajoharry. They told him to go to another place."

"To what other place did he go?"

"He has joined the preacher from Boston at Onoquaga on the Susquehanna. He sings many songs for that preacher and does only women's work. He is not a man any longer."

"It is good that this one lives in a far place," said Hanyost, struggling to strike the right tone in the Mohawk language. "Since he is not dead, when will my Mohawk brother return from the land of the Oneidas and Tuscaroras?"

Tekarihoga stood up suddenly, breaking off the conversation. "Here are the tools to be mended by the blacksmith."

Hanyost wondered if he had violated etiquette in some way by mentioning the return of Onatah from exile. Perhaps, he thought, more time is needed to make up for the act of violence. At least, he reasoned, Onatah no longer needed to fear a revenge attack by one of Dadawat's relatives.

During each of Hanyost's visits to the hearth of his friend's mother, Ataentsic stayed behind the deerskin curtain. One afternoon when the corn was growing high, Hanyost heard her cough. He thought that she was telling him that she knew he was there. He wondered how his friend's sister would find food for her new child, and he began to dream of taking Ataentsic and her baby, when it was born, to live in a lodge that he would build next to his mother's cabin.

11. The Sorrow of Ataentsic
June, 1772

Whenever Hanyost brought gifts of meat and fish to Onatah's mother, he looked for Ataentsic but he did not see her. Aware that he still did not fully understand the customs of the Mohawks, he assumed that she was in a time of seclusion. Later, he told himself, there will come a time when I may speak to her mother of my intentions. I am young, but among the people, I am of an age to become the husband of Ataentsic.

One morning in the time when the corn begins to grow tall, he brought a string of fish to Onatah's mother. She signaled for him to sit and began to speak.

"Brother of my son who is far away," she said. "The fish that you draw out of the river are very good."

"As you say it, mother-of-my-brother," responded Hanyost in Mohawk.

"Your true mother would enjoy such fish."

"You say truly," he answered. "I have caught enough fish for my mother's hearth and for this hearth of my brother's mother."

Onatah's mother was struggling to say something, and Hanyost understood that she was hampered by the formal courtesies of her language. Englishmen would have had no such difficulty, their language as crude and heavy as an ax to Hanyost's ears.

"The brother of my son brings too much meat and fish to this hearth," she tried again. Hanyost wondered if her relatives were embarrassed or angry that a white man brought food to a member of their family. He recalled a few unpleasant stares during recent visits to the village, but he attributed that to the growing friction between the tribe and the settlers.

"Mother-of-my-brother," said Hanyost. "You are saying that it is better if I no longer bring meat and fish to your hearth?"

She nodded, embarrassed. Hanyost nodded in return, searching for the right way to express himself in Mohawk. "Mother-of-my-brother, if there comes a time when you have need of me, I will be here. If ever there is a time when the sister of my brother has need of me, she has only to send word and I will come."

Onatah's mother looked directly at him, something she almost never did. She searched his eyes. She spoke with an unusual force. "My daughter Ataentsic has gone from this village. She went away five days after the child within her died"

"Died? The baby died? But where has she gone?"

"I am not sure." The mother's face, usually so placid, grew sad. "Some say that she has gone to the land of the Tuscaroras in search of her brother. Some say she has thrown herself into the river from the high cliffs near the little falls."

"She would not take her own life!" Hanyost was certain.

"You know her so well?" The face of Ataentsic's mother lightened.

"I think that I do."

"You have made my heart my glad with this saying."

"One day she will return to us."

"To us." The Mohawk woman smiled faintly. Hanyost returned her smile, and rose to leave.

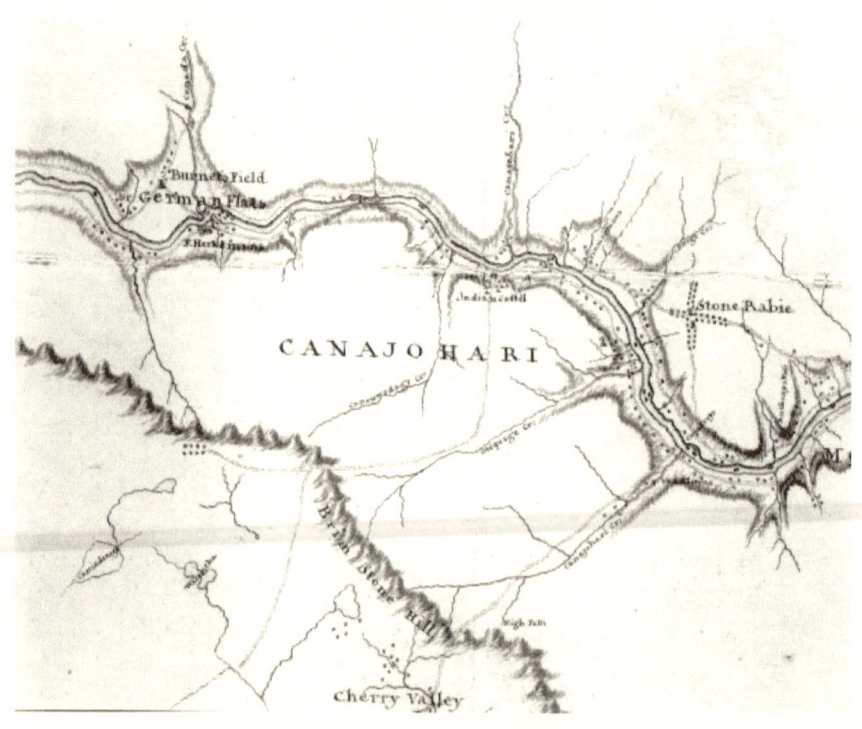

from the collection of the New York State Museum

1757 British map on which the entire south bank of the Mohawk from German Flatts to Stone Arabia is labeled "Canajohari," a variant spelling for the Mohawk Village. Present-day Canajoharie, NY is located on the eastern edge of this region.

12. The Ways of the Whites
Summer 1772 – December 1773

After learning that Ataentsic had gone away, Hanyost began to spend more time with the settlers. Still deeply influenced by Mohawk ways, he believed that he would find a special kinship with relatives on his mother's side. He sought out the children of his mother's sisters, and visited his Shoemaker and Bellinger cousins. However, he felt awkward among them and after a season, stopped coming by their farms.

Alone with his mother on their small farm, he became restless and visited most of the valley settlements, inquiring after the Mohawk girl of all whom he encountered, both Iroquois and white, but no one could answer him. He resolved to wait for her to return, certain that one day she would.

He grew closer to his mother, and began to share more of his feelings with her. She was sympathetic to his longing for the Mohawk girl, and urged him to be patient.

"There's many, my brothers and sisters included, who would frown mightily on a marriage between one of our family and an Indian girl, but I am not among them,' she told him. "Your father had a kind heart and was well disposed to the Mohawk people, and I know that he would say the same."

Elizabeth Schuyler had kept a kitchen garden for as long as Hanyost could remember, but she relied on her sewing and Nicholas' small income from his uncle for whatever cash needs they had. Unable to work the acres left to her by her husband, Elizabeth had rented much of the land to nearby settlers, in return for a small share of their corn.

Although Hanyost had provided well enough for his mother and himself through fishing and hunting small game, he realized that he was bringing in less and less meat from his days of hunting. Larger game animals were disappearing from the valley as the number of settlers increased, and now there seemed to be a decline in the numbers of rabbits and wild turkey. Even fish had become less plentiful as settlers set large nets upriver near Little Falls.

The time had come, Hanyost decided, to learn the ways of his own people, ways he had despised for so many years. He saw nothing that he could learn from his uncle, for Nicholas Herkimer relied on slaves to work his fields. Hanyost hated to see people who so closely resembled his old friend Jacob treated in this way. Even more, he did not want to see his own brother lording it over their uncle's slaves.

It was Hanyost's hope that he could find among the other settlers a teacher like Black Jacob, but his search was to be a disappointment.

"Dumm Hanyost," they called him and had much fun mocking his speech and unfamiliarity with their customs. To their ears, his oddly inflected German and his partly Iroquois vocabulary seemed ridiculous. After he had shown his willingness to work and to listen quietly to them, however, a few of the farmers grudgingly accepted his presence among them.

After studying the farms of each of the men in turn, he decided to offer his services to one of the more prosperous, Jacob Klock, who lived in a sturdy stone house in the middle of his hundred acres on the other side of the river. Hanyost admired his house, one of the finest he had ever seen, and the fields of newly sprouting corn.

A thrifty man, Klock did not reject Hanyost's offer of free labor, but he was puzzled by the many ways Hanyost had adopted from the Mohawks. His deerskin breeches and tunic, covered in Mohawk beadwork, seemed, in fact, to offend the farmer, but he had the strongest words for Hanyost's practice of covering his face, neck and hands with rancid bear grease.

"Keeps away the bugs," he told Klock, "Bug bites bring many sicknesses."

"That's crazy talk. All that grease does is make you smell like a dirty Injun!" Klock told him. The farmer assigned Hanyost the dirtiest jobs around his farm – hauling manure or slopping the pigs. "You smell bad, anyway and such chores won't make you stink any worse" was his comment.

Hanyost did not mind any task, as long as he learned something, and he observed each aspect of farm work very closely. By harvest time, Hanyost determined that he had learned all he could from Jacob Klock. He had a pocket full of seeds for the Spring, and a few ideas that he would try.

In the cold months that followed, Hanyost brought fresh game as far as Fort Herkimer or German Flatts, and after he had sold the meat, he would stand around in the tavern and listen to the men talk, hoping always for news of Ataentsic. They tolerated him, but always with a few jokes at his expense.

Hanyost heard stories of trouble far away in Boston, trouble with the king, but he did not understand much of what he heard.

"But why did the Boston men throw the tea into the harbor?" he asked Abel Hunt, only to provoke gales of laughter from the other men.

"Schuyler, you're too simple to worry about such things," laughed George Klock, for whose brother Hanyost had worked. "Politics is for white men, not Injuns, blacks or fools!"

13. An Old Deed
May, 1775

Over the years Hanyost had noticed that George Klock was always at the center of a loud group of local men. Ebenezer Cox, his brother-in-law, was often with him, as was Henry Nellis, a local trader.

Many years earlier Black Jacob and George had an angry confrontation. Hanyost had not witnessed the argument but, from what he heard in the village, Klock had been bragging about his legal rights to the land Connajoharry was built on. This was an old claim for Klock, one going as far back as the time of King Hendrick, who fell at Fort William Henry in 1757.

"The Tuscarora had never heard this lie, and he raised his stick as if to strike Klock down" is the way Tekarihoga described the incident. "But the Tuscarora was too old. He could not lift his arm high enough to strike."

"How can Klock tell such a lie?" Hanyost asked, saddened by the thought of his old friend.

"He has a worthless paper he bought from another white many years ago. The story is that the white was drunk and sold it to Klock for a few coins," Tekarihoga explained. "Since then Klock says he is the true owner of the land where we have built Connajoharry. Sir William told him many times that he is wrong and to shut his mouth, but Klock always returns to this old lie."

"But now Sir William is no longer in the land of the living."

"And white men like Klock are full of boldness. They talk of nothing but how their friends shot the redcoats in the towns of Concord and Lexington. Now Klock and the other thieves say they too will drive away the English and take what they want from us."

"Can nothing be done?"

"Maybe one of the warriors will kill him," said Tekarihoga. "Klock's tavern is close to the village, and he is selling rum to foolish braves. I think one of them will become maddened by drink and finally kill this old liar."

Knowing all this about Klock, Hanyost never entered his tavern. He recalled his Tuscarora friend's many warnings about strong drink when he saw Mohawks coming from Klock's place, staggering from the rum.

One morning in May, Hanyost was hurrying along the dirt road that led past the tavern. He was thinking about buying some hogs and knew that a farmer upriver had experience in raising and selling the animals.

Nearing Klock's tavern, Hanyost heard the sounds of a scuffle: raised voices, the crash of breaking crockery and the slap of fist on flesh.

"Who's he beating now?" wondered Hanyost, ticking off in his mind the possibilities: his wife, his son, one of his servants. Then he heard a moan and a plea for mercy, and realized that Klock himself was getting the beating this time. Unable to restrain his curiosity, Hanyost pushed open the tavern door. There he saw an unexpected sight.

Joseph Brant, the future war chief of the Mohawks, was administering a sound drubbing, English–style, to Klock, who was feebly attempting to hold up his own fists in defense. A half dozen braves, their arms folded, stood in the corners of the room, smiling as their leader got the best of the white man in his own game of fisticuffs.

"Oh, I'm nearly done, little white brother," said Joseph Brant in Mohawk, winking at Hanyost and driving his fist into Klock's jaw, administering a final kick that sent him sprawling across the floor. "This man would not shut his mouth about his right to the people's land."

The other Mohawks, although all of them knew him, eyed Hanyost with suspicion, but Brant quieted them with a gesture. "He is a friend of the true people," he told them. "We will go now."

Hanyost watched as the six Mohawks swiftly left the tavern, heading for Brant's property on the other side of Connajoharry.

Klock managed to get to his feet, sputtering with rage. "Brant had no right to beat me. I will get the law on him for assault."

Hanyost said nothing.

"Brant don't respect the law. None of these savages do, damn them!" The old man spat and rubbed his bruised jaw. "I have a deed, all proper and legal, that says I own their damned village. And when we throw out the Injun-loving English, I'll finally get some justice for my claim."

As Hanyost turned to go without a word, Klock called after him, "You feeble-minded simpleton, you don't understand a word I'm saying, do you?"

The very next day Hanyost was surprised to see Klock again, this time deep in conversation with his uncle. Unable to purchase a pair of hogs from other settlers, Hanyost had decided to swallow his pride and see if he could get a better price from Herkimer. He and his brother were walking back from the pig sty, where Nicholas had pointed out the two hogs that their uncle might be willing to sell.

Herkimer was in front of the manor house with several local men. Klock was there, his bruises from the previous day's beating visible from across the yard. Andy Fink, a close friend of Herkimer's and a prosperous farmer himself, was gesturing vigorously.

"This is one more reason why we need liberty!" Hanyost heard his uncle say. "So that disputes of this kind can be settled in fair-and-square courts. For too long Sir William was the only law in these parts. And now that his nephew Guy is the big man, it's no better."

"And have you heard how the Tory sheriff Alex White threw Adam Fonda in jail only for setting up a liberty pole?" asked Klock.

"We'll settle matters with him," Herkimer said. "I can't say too much, but there are plans afoot to gather a bunch of good lads and seize him by force."

"He deserves hanging, for sure," said Klock.

Catching sight of Hanyost, Andy Fink grabbed him by the arm, and thrust him in front of Herkimer "Here's a likely fellow for our militia, Nick. Your own sister's boy. Knows this country like the back of his hand. Speaks good Injun, too!"

"Oh, I'm not so sure," said Herkimer doubtfully. "My nephew is, you know..."

"Oh, he's a mite slow, I'll not deny that," said Fink. "But he's on good terms with the savages, ain't that so Hanyost? He could be just the man to help us talk 'em into coming in on our side, or at least staying out of the fight altogether."

Hanyost, thinking they were talking about the fight between Klock and Brant, and wanting to change the subject, said, "I went with Nicholas to see the pigs."

Herkimer laughed. "That's all right, lad. We'll see if we can get you and your ma a pair of hogs, and I'll give you better than a fair price."

His uncle clapped him on the shoulder and turned back to Klock. "Andy Fink and I have just come from a meeting of the Committee of Public Safety and we're riding up the valley to let folks know we need to organize our own militia."

"There's some in the county that'll stick with the King's men," warned Klock. "What are we to do with them?"

"I'll agree there's some that will not join us," said Herkimer, his eyes narrowing, "and we'll deal with 'em."

"But nearly all of us this side of Johnstown are very hearty in the present struggle for American liberty," he continued. "Ain't that right, George?"

"We sure are, Nick" said Klock. "It's time we drove out these Injuns and Englishmen."

"Now, now, George, this ain't just a fight for us white men to get Injun land," cautioned Fink. "It's for American liberty, and we want to try to get the tribes on our side. That's where fellas like Hanyost here could help us."

"But what about Brant? He got no right to come in my house, him and his five friends, and take turns beating me!"

"I am in agreement, George," said Herkimer. "We'll find a way to set this right."

"But Brant..." Hanyost wanted to refute Klock's lies about owning Connajoharry, but stopped himself. He realized that Herkimer must have heard Klock's story many times.

"What's that, boy?"

"Nothing, sir."

"Well, we have to spread the word up the valley," Herkimer concluded. "If we stand united, matters will be settled peacefully. If the King's men manage to divide us, I expect there'll be blood, just like over in Concord and Lexington last month."

Unable to pay even the low price Herkimer set for the breeding pair, Hanyost postponed his plan to raise pigs. He did settle on a price for a half dozen hens and a rooster, and went home to start work on a small coop for the fowl.

14. Buckskins & Arrows
Spring 1776

In the months that followed, Hanyost continued to visit the nearby farms and settlements to study the ways of farmers. He found the grist mill at Little Falls a good place to listen to his neighbors' conversation as they waited for their corn to be ground. Lingering at the edge of their circle, Hanyost paid close attention whenever local men discussed troubling news from beyond the valley.

In the Spring of 1776, he heard that Guy Johnson, who had succeeded his uncle Sir William as the king's representative to the Mohawks, had left his estate, Guy Park, with his family and servants and made for Canada. No one knew what side William's hotheaded son and heir, Sir John, would choose. But there was talk that he was raising a band of Indians to attack the settlers.

"The rich men like the Johnsons know which way the wind is blowing!" laughed Abel Hunt, who claimed to be active in the German Flatts Committee of Public Safety. "Even way out here in Indian country, we know what old King George is up to and we aim to defend American liberty and drive out all these big landowners."

"Will there be a fight, Abel?" another farmer asked.

"Oh, it's coming, it's coming," said Hunt, with the air of one who was in the know on these matters. "That's why Guy Johnson cleared out. Nick Herkimer and Ed Wall caught up with Guy at Cosby's farm and gave him a very firm letter explaining that we intended to stand by our country until all grievances were resolved. They asked him to help keep the savages neutral in this little dispute between us white men but Johnson would give them no satisfaction. He said that he was on his way to Canada and we had to deal with the Injuns on our own."

"And we'll deal with 'em, all right!" grinned George Van Deusen.

"We sure will," agreed Hunt. "Just look at how good old George Washington drove the redcoats out of Boston. And now he's fixin' to give 'em the same treatment in New York."

"But don't forget," said Van Deusen. "We have all those damned savages to worry about. Washington never had to deal with bloodthirsty heathen in Boston."

"What do the Injuns down at the castle say about this?" Hunt turned to Hanyost, who had remained silent. "You speak their language, right?"

"Yes."

"So what do they say? Will they join with the English and fight us?"

"I have not spoken with the Mohawks about these things," said Hanyost.

"But don't you go hunting with them regular?" Hunt persisted. "I hear you like to use a bow, like they do."

"No," said Hanyost. "I hunt alone."

"That's right," said one of the Snell brothers. "You only use a bow and arrow and they like their muskets better, don't they?"

"You're more of an Injun than they are," said Van Deusen, pointing to the flint knife at Hanyost's belt. "I bet none of them carry a stone knife like yours, leastways not in the past hundred years!"

Hunt stepped up to Hanyost and tapped his chest with his finger. "As a white man it's up to you to find out what them Injuns are thinking. Unless maybe you're a Tory sneakin' round here to spy on us?"

"A Tory?" Hanyost had never heard the term.

"A Tory. Someone who's a traitor to America and wants to help the English cut his neighbor's throats when the big fight comes. People like Guy Johnson and John Butler." The threat in Hunt's tone was unmistakable.

"I know nothing about these things." Hanyost backed away from Hunt.

"Ah, leave him alone, Abel," said Ebenezer Cox, who had just joined the group. "Hanyost is a simpleton. He can't do nothing for us." The rest of the men laughed.

From that day, Hanyost grew wary of his fellow white men. They all seemed eager for what they called a big fight with the Englishmen. The Mohawks whom he saw were noticeably less friendly, so he stayed to himself, tending to his farm. He was inordinately pleased with his first small crop of corn.

Hanyost hunted only for meat for himself and his mother and no longer went to sell game to the settlers. He avoided the gristmill and ground his own grain with a stone pestle. He became even more accurate with his bow and was able to stalk and kill with his flint-tipped arrows the ever rarer whitetail deer.

He dressed entirely in Mohawk buckskins and from time to time even wore an eagle feather in his long, braided hair. His brother Nicholas found Hanyost's increasingly eccentric ways an embarrassment and stopped visiting their mother at the cabin. Instead, Elizabeth went to her brother's house to see Nicholas and to sew for Herkimer's young second wife, Maria.

15. A Free Country
July 1776

When the corn was growing high, Nicholas made a rare visit to the cabin Hanyost shared with his mother, and mentioned that Herkimer had returned to his farm from Unadilla, full of imprecations against Joseph Brant. "Why?" asked Hanyost.

"Uncle Nick wanted to get the Mohawks on our side, and Joe Brant said no," replied Nicholas. "People are also saying that Nick planned to kill Joe if he couldn't get him to join up with the patriots."

"So, what happened?"

"The way I hear it, they both agreed on a parley at Unadilla and when they met, words got heated. Ebenezer Cox started to level his musket at Joe. Then the Mohawks all came out of the bushes, pointing their muskets at the militia."

"A standoff, then?"

"You could call it that."

"The two of them left on pretty bad terms, I guess?"

"Pretty bad."

"What do you think will happen next?" asked Hanyost.

"The way Uncle Nick sees it, the Johnsons will come down from Canada, join up with the Mohawks, and try to take back the whole valley. He says it'll be all-out war."

"Why will the Johnsons do such a terrible thing?"

"Why, Hanyost, don't you hear any news at all?" Nicholas shook his head in amazement. "Don't you know that we've declared our independence from old King George? Don't you know we're a free country now?"

"What does this mean?"

"It means that Ben Franklin and all the patriots met down in Philadelphia and drew up a paper telling the King that America is now a free country, that we don't have to pay no more taxes."

"And this is why the King's friends will come here to make war?"

"Of course! You don't think King George is just going to forget all that tax money and let us go without a fight, do you?"

"What will we do?" Hanyost looked to his mother, who seemed nearly as baffled as he.

"We have to defend our country, that's what we'll do," said Nicholas. "Uncle Nick won't let Johnson and his henchmen come back and make us all slaves!"

"Slaves? Like the black people on our uncle's farm?"

"Sure," said Nicholas. "The Englishmen and their savage friends want to make all us white people slaves just like the black ones are now."

"But how will our uncle stop them from doing this?" asked Hanyost, even more mystified.

Nicholas was surprised. "Haven't you heard about Uncle Nick's proclamation?"

"Proclamation? What is that?"

"Why, the General wrote a regular proclamation and had copies made and sent all over Tryon County. The paper says that the English are gathering up in Canada and every healthy man between sixteen and sixty is required to assemble at the proper place, armed and equipped to meet the invading forces. That's his exact words."

"Nick, are you going to fight?" His mother was alarmed.

"No, the General wants me to keep his farm running while he goes off to war. He has a big place, you know, and those slaves of his don't work without somebody keeping 'em on the job. "

"The soldiers will need food," Nicholas quickly added. "The General says it's just as important to keep the farm going as to fight the Tories."

"I understand," said his mother.

"But Uncle Nick thinks he's found a good position for Hanyost too," Nicholas said to their mother. "He'll be safe if trouble comes with the King's men.   And white folks around here will respect him instead of ..."

"I will not help you with the slaves," Hanyost insisted. "My grandfather-friend of the Tuscaroras said that the Creator does not permit any man to make a slave of another."

"No, our uncle knows how you feel about the slaves. Of course, he also knows that in the Good Book it says that slaves oughta be subject to their masters..."

"What does our uncle want me to do?" Hanyost cut short his brother's justification for slavery, which he had heard many times before.

"He says you could be a ranger."

"A ranger?"

"Yes, you would be officially listed as a ranger in one of the militia companies that are forming up, probably Hannes Demuth's outfit."

"Mr. Demuth lives out past German Flatts, does he not?"

"Yes, he does," said Nicholas. "But our uncle says that it'd be worth it for you to go out there and join up with his company. Hannes is easygoing and will let you do whatever kind of scouting you want to do. He's not a strict fellow, like Jacob Klock or Ebenezer Cox. Uncle Nick says that Hannes probably won't make you report when they get together for muster."

"What is muster?"

"Oh, marching around. Shooting off muskets, that sort of thing."

"I still do not understand."

"Uncle Nick says that Demuth would have employment more suited to your capacities. That's his words."

"What does our uncle mean by employment?"

"Well," Nicholas scratched his head. "I suppose he means the kind of work you would do for the militia."

"I will not shoot a musket." Hanyost was adamant.

"Uncle Nick knows that, Hanyost. That's why he wants you to go see Hannes Demuth, don't you see?"

"I still do not understand you." Anger rose in Hanyost's voice.

"All the companies have a few rangers attached to them, fellows like yourself who go off in the woods for days at a time, keeping their eyes open for signs of trouble from the Indians or Tories."

"The Mohawks are not my enemies."

"Uncle Nick knows that you're good friends with the Mohawks." Nicholas tried to be patient with his brother. "That's why he thinks that this employment will suit you just right."

"I will not fight against the Mohawk people!"

"But you won't have to fight!" Nicholas was losing his temper. "You just have to do whatever Captain Demuth tells you to do."

"Hanyost," Elizabeth intervened, not wanting to see her sons argue.

Hanyost turned toward his mother, inviting her opinion.

"I think you should do it, Hanyost," she said. "It sounds like you won't have to fight anyone. It will please my brother and will keep men like Hunt and Klock from bothering you."

"It's true," added Nicholas. "If that crowd thinks anybody is a Tory, they drive 'em out of the valley and take their land."

"If you wish this, mother," said Hanyost, "I will see Hannes Demuth and ask him to explain this work to me."

"I am glad," said his mother.

"But if these men do wrong, I will not stay with them."

16. Ranger for the Militia
summer 1776 – summer 1777

As a ranger for the militia, Hanyost found a role that suited him in these troubled times. Hannes Demuth, as Nicholas had said, was an easygoing man who enjoyed his pipe and beer.

"I'm right glad to have you in our regiment, Hanyost," said Demuth, pumping his hand. "I know you're not a man who cares for muskets but I'll have other work for you, you can be sure."

Recognizing that Hanyost would not take to the required drilling, Demuth allowed his new recruit wide latitude as to how he fulfilled his duties. "Just take your bow and arrows and stick close to your Mohawk friends, find out what they're thinking, and keep me informed of any treachery," he told Hanyost.

"The Mohawks are not my enemies," Hanyost insisted.

"I know that, boy. Don't worry yourself over that. You'll be helping your Mohawk friends this way. You won't be doing them any hurt."

"All right," Hanyost reluctantly agreed. "I will do good work for you."

"That's the spirit, my boy," Demuth shook his hand again. "You won't have anything to regret, I'm sure."

As Summer passed into Fall, Hanyost made his occasional visits to report privately to Captain Demuth at his farm and heard news of the war that raged beyond the still peaceful valley. General Washington had been driven out of New York and it seemed that the whole Continental Army was on the run. Then, when he saw Demuth a few days after Christmas, he learned that Washington had won a battle or two in New Jersey.

"Old George has got the king's hirelings on the run now!" gloated Demuth. "He gave the Hessians a good thrashing at Trenton, I'll tell you. Of course, it didn't hurt that the rascals were all drunk when he attacked!"

During the cold months, the main armies of the British and the Continentals were hunkered down in winter quarters. Travel among the settlements of the north was slow and difficult, but Demuth knew that the Indians could move swiftly no matter what the season. He and the other militia officers feared a surprise attack.

At January's regular meeting with Hanyost, the captain had a new assignment for him, one that he believed only Hanyost could fulfill.

"My boy," he began, "I appreciate the news you've been bringing me from the Mohawks. As long as Molly Brant and her friends stay at Connajoharry and avoid chatting with Tories, I think we can feel confident that her brother isn't cooking up trouble."

"The Mohawks will not talk much to me," said Hanyost, "but Molly Brant talks to my mother, and she says nothing of helping the Englishmen in their war."

"Good!" Demuth offered a stein to Hanyost. "I think we can count on the savages in Connajoharry staying quiet for now. But there's another place I want you to go take a look at."

"Yes?"

"Do you know where Unadilla is?"

"Yes." Hanyost knew most of the old Indian paths and had hunted to within a few miles of the settlement at the fork of the Susquehanna.

"Could you sneak up on Unadilla in your snowshoes, and take a look at the town for me?"

"I could."

"You see, Unadilla has become the main stronghold of the Tories and Brant's Mohawks. If they are going to attack the valley settlements, they will need to gather there. I want you to go take a look, see who's going and coming, and discover if they're building up supplies for war. Muskets and powder and the like. Can you do that?"

"Yes." Hanyost rose to prepare for the journey.

"You don't say much, my boy," said Demuth, grasping his shoulder, "You're like an Injun that way. But I know I can count on you."

Throughout the winter and into the spring of 1777, Hanyost kept a careful watch over events at Unadilla. More than once he had strolled into the town to sell game to the townsmen. He saw several Mohawks whom he knew and listened closely to them. Since the Mohawks accepted his presence, the whites tended to see him as a Tory.

He learned that the Indians and the local whites did expect that there would eventually be an attack upon those they called "the rebels." But Hanyost saw no immediate signs of preparation for war, and reported all this to Demuth.

As the growing season began, Hanyost concentrated on planting his corn crop and did not return to Unadilla. "I will go soon," he told himself, but there always seemed to be one more task he had to complete.

By the beginning of August, Hanyost finally felt that his corn crop would be safe if he were absent for a few days, and made ready to depart for Unadilla. Rain had been plentiful and the first shoots were growing rapidly into tall green plants. He expected the best harvest ever, and looked forward to an easing of his and his mother's chronic poverty. "Soon" he told his mother, "we will be rich farmers and you will not need to ruin your eyes sewing for Uncle Nick's young wife."

"Oh Hanyost," replied Elizabeth. "I enjoy Maria's company."

"Perhaps you do, mother," conceded Hanyost. "But with this corn crop coming in, we will have enough money at last. You will be able to buy whatever you want!"

Hanyost embraced his mother. "Just keep an eye on the corn while I'm gone. Be sure that no one's pigs get into our field."

"But where are you going?" asked his mother.

"I must be off to Unadilla for the captain. I should have gone earlier, but I am sure there is no trouble there. Unadilla has been quiet all winter. In fact, I am beginning to think that there will be no war in our valley."

"I pray that it may be so."

"But I am pledged to the captain to go, and I must."

Hanyost set to gathering his supplies for the journey, and was soon off. He decided to visit Connajoharry first, just to assure the captain that no mischief was brewing there.

As he approached the Mohawk village, Hanyost noticed how sadly neglected it appeared. Many Mohawks had already gone off to Unadilla or to Canada and mostly women, children and old men remained in the village. The once prosperous fields were badly overgrown and only a few stands of corn, beans and pumpkin sprouted among the weeds. All the old longhouses but one looked abandoned, with holes in their bark roofs. The walls of the hastily thrown-together plank cabins were sagging.

Coming past the dilapidated palisades, he was surprised to see a crowd of white men emerging from one of the seemingly abandoned longhouses, carrying a few iron kettles and farm tools. Among them he saw the stout figure of old George Klock.

"You men," Hanyost called out, his anger rising at the sight of Klock. "Why are you here?"

"Oho, look George," called one of the men. "It's the idiot Hanyost."

"Why are you in the longhouse?" demanded Hanyost. "Why are you taking those things?"

"This is my property now," crowed Klock. "I have the deed and there's no damned redcoat like Johnson to deny me my rights!"

A woman's voice rang out. "You are a thief and a liar, Klock!"

Hanyost turned to see the stately figure of Molly Brant advancing, her eyes blazing with anger. Several Mohawk women were by her side. "You would not dare to do this if my brother were here!"

"Your brother!" guffawed Klock. "Do you mean the Tory traitor and butcher Joe Brant? We'll hang him high when we catch him."

Molly Brant quickly closed the distance between herself and the white men and struck Klock a resounding slap in his face.

"You witch!" cried Klock, trying to strike her back. "I'll teach you not to hit a white man."

Hanyost slammed into Klock, knocking him to the ground. One of the other white men struck Hanyost a glancing blow to the head while a second raised a flintlock pistol and fired. The shot went wild and Hanyost wrestled the weapon from the man and clubbed him to the ground.

The Mohawk women leaped onto the white men, punching and scratching. Finally, with their superior numbers, the Indian women had pinned the four men to the ground. One of them had a knife and was about to stab Klock when Hanyost seized her arm and held her back.

"Stop, all of you!" he shouted. "This is wrong. Men must not fight women."

The fighting ceased as quickly as it had started.

"Now, go away," Hanyost shouted. "Leave this village now."

Embarrassed, Klock's companions struggled to their feet.

"Leave but first give back all that you have stolen."

Klock, sputtering with rage, did not move.

"Leave this place. Now!" ordered Hanyost "Before these women kill you."

"You'll regret this, you Tory scoundrel," snarled Klock. "The day is coming when we'll hang all you Tories."

"I am a ranger for the militia, you coward," said Hanyost. "What have you done for the patriot cause except try to steal from women and children?"

"You'll regret this," repeated Klock. Hanyost moved toward him, but his companions grabbed the old man and backed away, cursing.

"And don't come back!" Hanyost shouted after them as they retreated from the Mohawk village. He threw the flintlock pistol after them. "And take your filthy weapon with you."

"I have a deed," Klock called out from beyond the palisade. "I own this whole village and when we win this war, I mean to have it!"

17. Molly Brant's Letter
August 2, 1777

"Thank you, Hanyost." Molly Brant touched his arm. "It is good to have at least one warrior left in this poor village."

"Klock is a bad man. I could not let him steal from you."

"Come and join us at our meal," said Molly.

"I have a task to do. I must be going."

"Please stay," insisted Molly. "You know the ways of our people. And you know that we must honor you for your help."

Taking him by the arm, Molly led Hanyost into her longhouse. The other women followed.

Entering the lodge, Hanyost marveled at how well kept it was. English-style tables and chairs were in evidence, as were the traditional Mohawk mats and sleeping pallets. On the wall he saw an oil painting of Molly's late husband, Sir William, alongside intricately carved wooden masks of the False Face Society. He knew that in the old days, such masks were kept carefully hidden until needed to frighten away the spirits who brought illness. Molly, however, had arranged objects from both cultures to suit her own taste.

As they sat before the fire, he noticed how well dressed she was, and how young she still seemed. Her dress was of pale blue cotton and around her slender waist she wore an artfully beaded deerskin belt. Her golden earrings sparkled in the dim light.

Molly smiled gently at him. "When you defended us, you reminded me of my brother. You have his courage."

Hanyost, blushing, was unsure how to answer.

Molly signaled to one of the women to bring a glass of wine to Hanyost. He sipped at it, admiring the thin stemmed glass.

"Do you like the wine?" she smiled. "I learned to enjoy this drink at Sir William's house. When his white family made me and my children leave Johnson Hall, I brought a few bottles with me, to share only with those who are truly friends."

"I have never tasted wine before."

"Tell me, Hanyost," Molly said slowly. "Are you truly a ranger for the militia?"

"I am."

"Would you fight with the militia against our people?"

"That would never happen."

"You think not?"

"No, the militia is only to protect us if the Englishmen come here with their armies, as they did at Boston and New York."

"What task does the militia have for you?"

Hanyost hesitated. He well knew that Hannes Demuth was suspicious of Molly Brant. After all, much of his own work for the militia was to keep an eye on her people in Connajoharry and, since last winter, in Unadilla.

"Captain Demuth has asked me to go on what he calls patrols."

"What does that mean?"

"I go on long journeys through the forest and make sure that no enemies are approaching the valley."

"Have you found any such enemies?"

"No, all is quiet. And this I have told to my captain, Hannes Demuth."

Molly took the glass from Hanyost's hand and sipped from it. She handed it back to him. "Sir William had this wine brought from France."

"Where is France?"

"Across the great water. Near to England."

One of the other Mohawk women approached and whispered to Molly. "Come, Hanyost," she said, rising from the fireside. "Let us sit at the table and eat together. My friends have made a savory dish of rabbit and herbs for you to enjoy."

As they came to the beautifully polished oak table, Hanyost noticed the elegant china plates and silver eating utensils. "These things also I brought from Johnson Hall," explained Molly. "Please, sit."

Hanyost was unaccustomed to forks and had some difficulty picking up one of the small pieces of rabbit. "This is very good," he said.

"Without warriors, we must make do with whatever small animals we women can catch."

"When do you think that your brother and the other warriors will be able to return to the valley?" asked Hanyost.

"When the danger of war has passed." A sorrowful expression clouded Molly Brant's face.

"When will that be?"

"Soon, I hope." She looked up, forcing a faint smile.

"Then you do not think there will be fighting between the true people and the settlers?"

"It is my hope that there will be no war here in our valley," she said. "There are many good people who want peace."

"Good," said Hanyost. "I am glad. If our two peoples were to fight, what side would I be on?"

"I think that in your soul you are one of us, Hanyost." She was very serious. After a moment of silence, she continued. "Do you remember the wise man of the Tuscarora, the one whom the English called Black Jacob?"

"Of course. He taught me many skills."

"Black Jacob was my friend also. He once told me that in the land he came from, there were many white men who wished to make slaves of the red people just as they did of the black people. He told me that he could see this desire in the eyes of all whites who kept slaves."

Hanyost nodded. The same thought had occurred to him. "The Creator is angry when one man makes a slave of another."

"I have seen the slaves of your uncle Nicholas Herkimer working in his fields." Molly paused, looking closely at Hanyost. "Did you know that the King has forbidden men to keep slaves in England?"

"I did not know this."

Molly took another sip from the glass of wine.

"The wise Tuscarora also spoke of you."

"What did he say?" Hanyost leaned forward across the table.

"He said that you were truly Iroquois in your heart. He said that you were more like the warriors of his time than the young men of the tribes who want only to live like the whites."

"I am glad to hear this."

"Black Jacob also told me that one day you would do a great thing for both our peoples."

"What thing did he say I would do?"

"He said that you would come to us and I would know when the day came."

Hanyost was puzzled. "I do not understand."

"Today is that day of which your grandfather-friend spoke." Molly took both his hands in hers.

"Today is the day when you will do the great thing of which he spoke."

"But what can I do?"

"You can be the one to prevent bloodshed between our two peoples."

"But how?"

"Listen carefully to me." Her dark eyes did not waver from his. "You know that I have many friends among both peoples, from when I was the mistress of Johnson Hall, the chief lady of all the northern borderlands."

Hanyost nodded.

"I have learned that the King and George Washington have made an agreement to bring an end to the war in a way that will satisfy all of the people of this land and of England. The Americans will have all the liberties which they could desire and the King will receive the honors that matter so much to him. All will be well and there will be no bloodshed between our two peoples."

"This is good news!" exclaimed Hanyost. "I must tell my captain, Hannes Demuth, and my uncle of this!"

"No, Hanyost, you must not do that."

"But why not?"

"It is true that the King and General Washington have made an agreement for peace. But there are other men who want war, men like George Klock."

"So that they can steal land from the Iroquois people!"

"Yes, and make slaves of them as they do of the black people."

"How can such evil men be stopped?"

"There may be a way, Hanyost. Those who are in the militia do not yet know of the peace agreement. Those who want war have sent out false orders bearing the forged signature of General Washington. One of the men who has been deceived by these lies is Nicholas Herkimer."

"I will explain to him!"

"No, Hanyost. You know that he will not listen to you. He does not understand how much you know. Like the other whites, your uncle thinks that you are stupid."

Although hurt, Hanyost had to agree. "He might listen to my brother but you are right. My uncle thinks I am a fool."

"But there is still a great thing you can do to save us all from war."

"What can I do?"

"Let me explain. These false orders tell your uncle to take the militia and march west to attack the good Iroquois and whites who have gathered for a peace conference at Fort Stanwix."

"I have not heard of such orders." Hanyost felt a moment of doubt.

"The militia will be called to muster tomorrow."

"But what can be done?"

"Your uncle Johan Herkimer, is there at the peace conference. Johan and many good people from the valley have been meeting with my brother and with my stepson, Sir John. They have all voted to have peace."

She touched his hand.

"Men like Klock want to have the militia break up the conference. They want to burn the villages of the Oneidas and Tuscaroras and kill all, even the women and children. You know that Klock and his kind are capable of this."

Hanyost stood up, pacing back and forth in his anxiety. Molly continued. "But if the good people learn of this impending attack, they will cross over the lake Ontario and avoid the battle. If they can avoid a battle even for a few days, there will be time for the true messengers of the King and General Washington to spread word of the peace agreement, and all will be well. And this is why I need you to carry a message to the peace gathering at Fort Stanwix."

"You want me to carry a message?"

"Yes, to your uncle Johan."

"My uncle Johan?

"Like you, he is a man in whom I have trust."

Going to a cherrywood cabinet, Molly took paper and quill and began to write quickly. Looking up once, she asked, "Can you read?"

His face red, Hanyost admitted that he could not. "But I can write my name."

"No matter. I only wanted to ask you if I was using the right word." Finishing the letter, she dripped wax from a nearby candle and stamped it with her signet ring. "If you go straight west along the river, you will meet the good people at the portage place where the waters begin to flow toward the Great Lakes. Is that a country where you usually patrol for Captain Demuth?"

"No, I patrol south to the Susquehanna."

"But you must have a credential, a piece of writing to show other patrols if you are stopped. A paper that proves that you are a ranger for the militia and not a Tory."

"Yes." Hanyost touched the leather pouch at his waist. "I carry it here. But when I enter a village like Unadilla, I hide it in the woods so that the Tory men will not find it if they search me."

"On this journey you must carry the credential, so that if militia men stop you, you can explain that you are on a special mission for your captain."

"But Captain Demuth…"

"Listen, Hanyost." Molly handed him the letter. "If you can carry this to your uncle, you will save many, many lives. If you fail, thousands will die. The whole valley will be in flames. You must not fail."

"I will not fail," said Hanyost. "I will deliver this letter to my uncle Johan."

Molly touched the deerskin belt that encircled her slender waist. Hanyost saw that its design was carefully embroidered in purple and white. "This was a gift sent to me by my young cousin, Ataentsic."

"Ataentsic!" All of his feelings for the girl came rushing back. "Then you have heard from her? Where is she?"

"I believe that she has joined with the good people who seek peace."

"Then she is with Uncle Johan? I will see her there?"

"I cannot be sure, but I believe she is with them. She is much respected by the people as a healer."

Embracing him, Molly told Hanyost, "You are a true warrior of the Mohawk people. I know that you are the one who Black Jacob prophesied would bring peace to both our peoples."

18. The Deserter

Hanyost waded across Nowadaga Creek, shallow in summer, and passed the cornfields of his uncle. He was eager now to reach the Iroquois and their friends in the west, and feared being discovered and stopped by militia patrols. Deciding that it would be safer to avoid the busy road that followed the narrow river valley west to the portage at Little Falls, he cut across wooded country and began to climb the slopes of Fall Hill. From its summit he would be able to observe the road to German Flatts, and decide how best to choose his path to Oneida country.

The day was hot and humid, and the mosquitoes plentiful. As he neared the brow of the hill, Hanyost paused to rest and looked through a clearing in the trees down upon the valley. Even compared to five years earlier, when he and Onatah had made their way westward in a fierce blizzard, the valley had greatly changed. Settlers' cabins and cleared fields covered the hillsides beyond the river, and wagon traffic was heavy on the main road from Schoharie country to German Flatts. Heavier than most days, Hanyost noted.

Looking back downriver, he saw his uncle's spacious brick home set among ripening fields of corn and wheat. A few tiny figures, probably slaves, worked in the fields. A number of wagons and an unusual number of men were gathered at the front entrance to the farmstead. Near the barn he saw a man grooming his uncle's white horse. Even at that distance, Hanyost recognized his brother Nicholas.

Perhaps there is news, thought Hanyost. Have the messages of peace from General Washington and King George arrived?

Curious and wishing to avoid a long and unnecessarily circuitous route to the west, Hanyost turned back and began to quickly descend the hillside.

Approaching the house from the barn side, Hanyost found Nicholas still brushing the general's beautiful horse. "Our uncle must think very well of you, brother, to let you take care of such a horse."

Startled, Nicholas seized his arm and pulled him into the shadow of the barn, away from the front entrance of the house. "Hanyost!" his brother whispered. "Are you crazy? What are you doing here?"

"What do you mean?"

"Uncle Nick heard that you deserted to the Tories!"

"What?" Hanyost was nearly speechless.

"Sure enough. In fact, he sent a letter to General Schuyler in Albany, reporting that you and a half dozen other fellas, Uncle Johan and Peter Tenbrook among 'em, deserted the militia and cut out for Canada." Nicholas peeked nervously around the corner of the barn. "If they see you here they'll hang you sure enough. That's what they say they're gonna do to all the Tories they catch."

"Why would our uncle do this to me?" Hanyost was angry and baffled. "I am a good ranger for the militia. I do everything that Captain Hannes Demuth asks me. I brought him reports of the Tories at Unadilla all winter."

"I don't know about Demuth," said Nicholas. "From what I hear, he ain't even a captain any more. Not since Uncle Johan cut out for Canada.

That whole Kingsland regiment is gone to pieces now and they say Demuth sits home and don't know what to do."

"I do not understand."

"You do know that Uncle Johan was going to be in charge of the Kingsland regiment, don't you?

"I only know Captain Demuth. I brought my reports to him at his farm. He told me I do not have to go to muster and march around."

"Maybe Demuth was a traitor, too. That's all I know."

"But who told Uncle Nick that I joined the Tories?"

"Old George Klock is the one that brought the word. Seems he had spies in Uncle Johan's gang, so he got the news right away."

"Klock! Of course! Now it is clear to me."

"I hear he and his brother Jacob even set out to catch Uncle Johan and the other deserters as they headed north to Oswego. But they lost their trail."

"Klock hates me, ever since I saw Joseph Brant beat him in his tavern. It is Klock who made up this lie about me. And my own uncle believed him! He did not even bother to walk over to our farm and ask me if it was true."

"I don't know about any of that," cautioned Nicholas. "But you are in danger here, especially since the word came from Fort Stanwix to raise the militia."

"What do you mean?"

"Why, haven't you heard?"

"Heard what?"

"That the British General St. Leger has come down from Oswego with a big force of redcoats, joined by Tories and Joe Brant's Injuns, and laid siege to the fort. Colonel Gansevoort made a desperate plea for help and Uncle Nick has sent word that every man in the militia is to report to Fort Dayton tomorrow and get ready to march over to Fort Stanwix and drive off the redcoats and their friends."

"This is very bad news." Hanyost quickly compared what his brother told him to Molly's description of the plot to undo General Washington's peace plan. It was obvious to him that George Klock had done just what Molly feared. He had forged orders to Uncle Nicholas in order to cause a battle that would end all hopes of peace.

"I must go now." Hanyost's mind was set. As Molly had said, it was up to him, and him alone, to bring her vital message to Uncle Johan and the others gathered near Fort Stanwix.

"Where will you go?"

"I am a ranger, Nicholas. I am still a ranger for the militia and I know what I must do."

Clasping his brother's hand, Hanyost turned and hurried back into the nearby woods, circling around to avoid any contact with the growing crowd of men at his uncle's house. Climbing over Fall Hill, he descended to the river by nightfall and found a canoe tied up near a settler's cabin just beyond the rapids. Silently pushing it into the dark waters of the river, he began to paddle westward against the slow current.

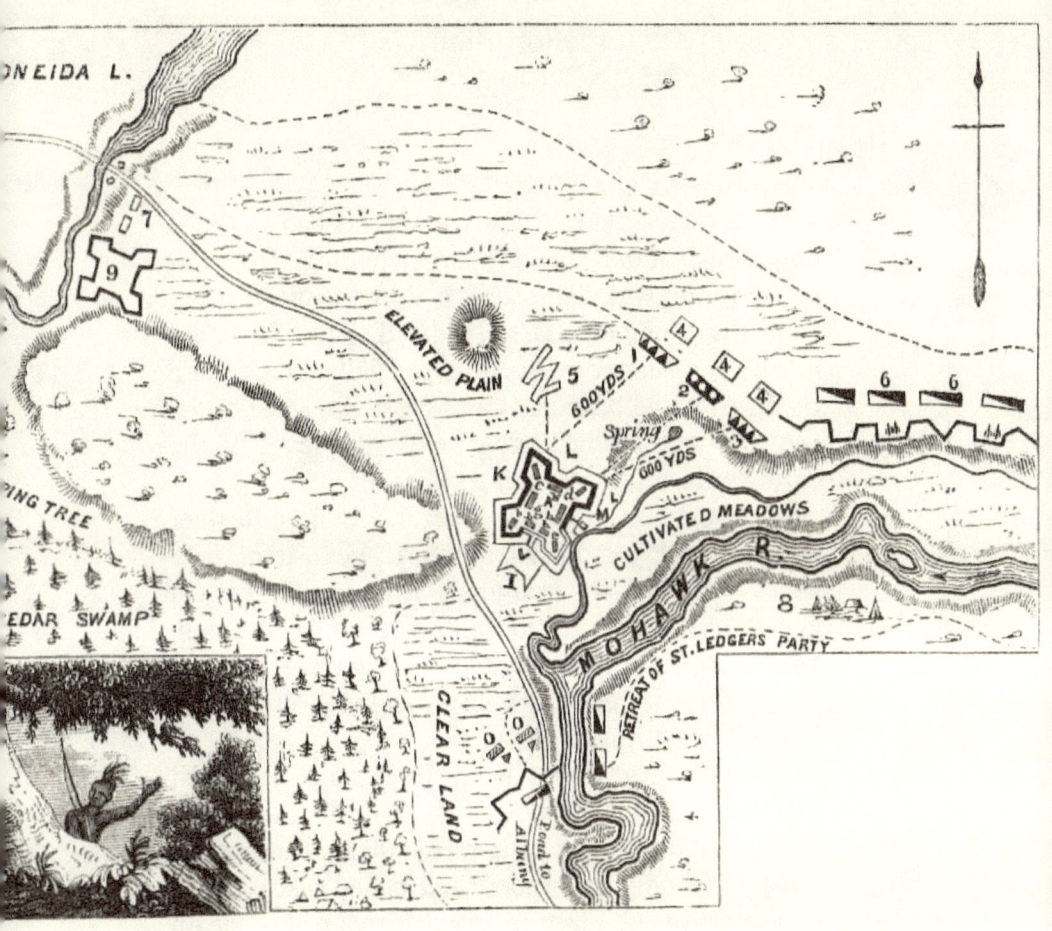

Map of Fort Stanwix from *Pictorial Field Book of the Revolution* by
Benson J. Lossing, 1859

19. Fort Stanwix
August 4, 1777

Two days later, Hanyost crouched in the underbrush at the edge of a large clearing. The early morning air was damp and a thin fog was lifting from the trampled grass. In the distance he could make out a banner with red stripes and a blue square flying from the bastion of Fort Stanwix. Most of the fort was not visible, lying below the level of the earthworks and surrounding palisades.

Hanyost felt Molly's letter, safe in a leather pouch under his buckskin shirt. Less than fifty paces away, he saw Iroquois warriors milling about as soldiers, some in red coats and some in green, tended cooking fires. He noted that the tents seemed of good quality and the men's muskets were staked in a military fashion.

Lookouts had been posted along the portage trail leading from the Mohawk River to Wood Creek, but he had managed to creep past them. The guards, mostly Iroquois, were alert and it had taken him a good part of the night to crawl forward this far on his hands and knees.

Hanyost had heard no sound of gunfire as he slowly approached Fort Stanwix, but his first sight of the lookouts signaled to him that hostilities were expected. He hoped that Klock's evil scheme had not yet been put into motion.

After watching the camp for nearly an hour, he decided to reveal himself.

Rising and stepping out into the clearing, Hanyost raised his bow above his head with both hands, a sign of peaceful intention among the

Iroquois. Immediately, the warriors and soldiers saw him and trained their weapons on him.

"I come in peace," Hanyost called out in Mohawk, repeating the same words in English. "I come bearing a message for my uncle, Johan Herkimer."

Two Iroquois warriors, probably Seneca, were the first to reach him, their tomahawks raised to strike.

"I raise my bow in the sign of peace," said Hanyost in Mohawk, not sure if they understood the dialect. "I place my bow upon the ground."

By this time, two soldiers, one in an unbuttoned red jacket, were at his side. "How did you get here?" demanded the redcoat. "How did you get past our pickets?"

"I am a friend of the Mohawks. From them I have learned to move quietly in the forest."

"You have learned well, old friend."

The voice was a familiar one. Hanyost recognized Joseph Brant and took his extended hand. Brant explained quickly to the Senecas that Hanyost was a friend. "Come," he said. "We must go first to the British commander, St. Leger. Then we will see your uncle."

Followed by a small crowd of curious Iroquois, Brant led Hanyost toward the largest of the military tents, set up in a small hollow beyond gunshot of the fort. He saw the familiar flag of the English king flying before the tent.

"What message is it that you bring for your uncle?" asked the Mohawk leader.

"Your sister Molly wrote a letter for me to bring to him," explained Hanyost. "She has learned that evil men like George Klock have lied to my Uncle

Nicholas and persuaded him to bring the militia to attack the peace conference."

"Peace conference?" Brant looked sidelong at him in puzzlement. "Is this what my sister's letter says? Did you read it?"

Hanyost shook his head in embarrassment. "I cannot read. Your sister told me the words that she was putting into the letter. But I must give the paper to my Uncle Johan."

"I see." A look of understanding flashed across Brant's face. "General St. Leger is obliged to read all such messages, you understand. It is a military requirement, and I am sure that your Uncle Johan would want the general to see the letter first. Do you have it?"

"It is in this pouch."

"Good." Brant placed his hand on Hanyost's shoulder. "Here is the general's headquarters."

Brushing past the two sentries, Brant led Hanyost into the spacious tent. "Good morning, general!" he called out. "Here's a document I think you'll wish to peruse."

A tall thin Englishman, in his shirt and suspenders, was being shaved by a servant. He looked up in annoyance, flinching as the servant's razor nicked him. "Damn!" he muttered, reaching for a towel to wipe away the soap from his face. "Why can't you wait to be announced like everyone else, Captain Brant?"

"My apologies, general," Brant smiled. "But I believe that you need to see this document straightaway."

He motioned for Hanyost to hand the letter to the angry general.

"Why can't any of you Provincials learn to salute?" he said wearily to Hanyost, taking the folded paper and breaking the wax seal. "You will never learn how to be soldiers."

"He's not one of the King's Royal Regiment of New York," explained Brant. "But he has come from Connajoharry with a message of some import."

Carefully reading the letter, St. Leger frowned. "This is from your sister, Molly Brant."

"So this young man told me."

"And it's addressed to Johan Herkimer."

"I thought that you should read it first, sir."

"Quite right." He read it through again, more slowly. "Do you know what it is that she writes?"

"No sir, I do not."

"I know that it is a warning," Hanyost burst out. "That bad men want to destroy the plans for peace of General Washington and good King George."

"Who is this fellow?" St. Leger stepped closer and looked intently at Hanyost. "He's surely does not know his place. And what is he talking about?"

"Hanyost grew up close to my people. The whites say he is mad, but we know him for a man of much wisdom. He is also the nephew of Johan Herkimer and of the traitor Nicholas Herkimer."

"Molly Brant gave you this letter?"

"Yes."

"What's all this about the traitor Washington and King George?"

"They want peace and bad men want war."

"Much wisdom. This man surely has much wisdom," said St. Leger, tapping his forehead and winking at Brant. Handing the letter to the Mohawk chief, he asked "Is this your sister's handwriting?"

"Yes, it is written in her hand." Brant quickly scanned the letter. "And the warning she gives us is most timely, you will agree."

"What kind of a force can Herkimer mount against us, if he does try to break the siege?"

"He'll come with eight hundred, maybe even a thousand men."

"So many as that?"

"But an undisciplined mob, all militia and not a true soldier among them. We can easily lay an ambush and cut them to pieces, and I know just the spot."

"Ambush?" Hanyost was alarmed. "I must talk to my Uncle Johan. He will understand what Molly Brant says. He will understand that you must not fight."

"I think it's time to send your young friend out to get breakfast, Captain Brant," said St. Leger. "He's clearly an ideal messenger but I don't think we need him in our war council, do you?"

"Hanyost, would you wait for me outside the tent?"

"I must take this letter to my Uncle Johan." Hanyost reached for the letter in Brant's hand.

"No, it's too valuable for you to carry about any longer, but you have done brave work bringing it this far," Brant said soothingly. "Now, go outside and ask the men where you can find your Uncle Johan."

Hanyost considered Brant's suggestion for a moment before going out through the tent flap. Tekarihoga, whom he knew well from Connajoharry, was waiting for him. "They told me that you were here, old friend," said the Mohawk. "You have walked far and must share food at our fire. Come."

"Not yet," replied Hanyost, "I need to find Johan Herkimer, the brother of my mother. He is in this camp."

"I will accompany you and we will find the brother of your mother," answered Tekarihoga.

As they walked along past the tents, the Mohawk reminisced about Connajoharry. "I remember well the winter games on the frozen river with your brother-friend Onatah."

"Have you heard any word of my brother-friend?"

"It saddens my heart to say that Onatah, like many of his adopted people, the Oneidas, fights against the King."

"And his sister Ataentsic? Have you had word of her?"

"She is a great healer."

"I, too, have heard this." Hanyost was eager for news of the Mohawk girl. "Do you know where she is?"

"Ataentsic is here in the camp," said Tekarihoga. "When Thayendenegea, the one the whites call Joseph Brant, led us to meet with St. Leger at Oswego nine days ago, she was already there."

"Is she with a husband now?" Hanyost was eager for more news. "Does she have children?"

"No, she was without a man. She traveled with women friends from the Cayuga and Onondaga peoples, all known among their people as healers. They joined us on the march from Oswego and were with us when we first came to this fort four days ago. Then Gansevoort with great pride rejected the offer of peace made to him by St. Leger's man, Lieutenant Bird. They fired their muskets instead of talking and two Mohawks were badly wounded. Ataentsic cared for them and both still live."

"I would speak with her," Hanyost said. "Where is she now?"

"Yesterday she went out, seeking healing herbs in the forest with her women friends. She has not yet returned."

"Tell me, why did Gansevoort and his men fire their muskets?"

"Why would they not? Their fort is strong and they will not surrender it to us."

"But the peace talks? I have been told that both sides came here to make peace talks and bring an end to the war among the whites."

"This is a strange saying, friend of our people. I have heard of no peace talks. We came here to destroy the fort and all who are in it. Then we will go down the river and join with the other great army of the King that comes from Montreal under the chief Burgoyne and destroy all the traitor men."

"My uncle Johan Herkimer knows of this plan for war?"

The Mohawk stopped walking and looked directly at Hanyost. After a pause he spoke, "I do not know of all these things. You will find Johan Herkimer there." He pointed toward a line of entrenchments over toward the fort. "But be wary of musket balls from those in the fort."

"Could Molly be so mistaken?" he murmured to himself. Just then, he heard the report of a musket. Looking toward the fort, he saw black smoke drifting from one of the bastions. Then another musket fired.

"Down! You fool, get down!"

Hanyost dropped to the ground, and saw who had warned him. Uncle Johan!

A rattle of musket fire from the Tories and redcoats whistled over his head toward the fort. Then, as he raised his head slightly to look about, Hanyost was buffeted by a nearby explosion. A small brass cannon had fired toward the fort. It did not seem to make any appreciable impact on the walls but was followed by another cannon blast from farther down the trench.

"What in salvation are you doing here, boy?" His uncle motioned him to crawl forward toward a fortified earthwork. "And keep your head down. The rebels have a couple of good sharpshooters up there."

Hanyost peeked through a cut in the timber and earthen wall to get a better view of the fort. Open ground sloped upward toward an outer line of palisades, effectively shielding all but the very top of the fort from musket or cannon fire. Anyone attempting to storm the fort would have to run upward against fire from two diagonal walls of horizontal logs.

"I had a letter for you," he said to his uncle. "Molly Brant wrote it."

"Molly Brant?" Another musket shot rang out and his uncle pulled Hanyost away from the opening. "Keep down, I tell you! Two days ago we had one of our boys drilled right through the eye, a Frenchman he was, down from Montreal."

"Molly Brant said that I was to give the letter to you. But Joseph Brant took the letter to the English general."

"Why would Joe Brant's sister write to me? We are not exactly the best of friends."

"She told me that you were here to join in peace talks that would end the war. She said that all of you were gathered here at the fort for such talks. And that evil men plotted to attack so that the war would not be ended."

"Sounds like flummery to me, lad. There's no peace talks here, as you can plainly see."

"Do you think that Molly Brant did not speak the truth to me?"

"Well, let me say this, lad. You wouldn't be the first man that Molly, with her fetching ways and darling figure, has deceived!"

From *The Pictorial Field Book of the Revolution* by Benson Lossing, 1859

20. Treasonous Intent
August 5, 1777

Hanyost spent an uneasy night, trying to sleep on the floor of the tent his uncle shared with several other men who had deserted with him from the militia. All through the previous day he had remained at his uncle's side, laboring with a pick and shovel to extend the entrenchment farther toward the fort.

"The Injuns refuse to do this kind of work," muttered Peter Tenbrook, an irascible middle-aged man who had deserted the American militia with Johan. "They say this is slaves' work, fit only for the blacks, and I'll agree with 'em."

"Are you regretting coming here?" Hanyost asked, straining to pry up a large rock that blocked their way.

"No, boy." Tenbrook wedged a branch behind the rock to help pull it out of the earth. "No, I don't regret it even with all our slaving now. When Joe Brant and his friends finish off that lot of hypocrites in the valley, we'll be enjoying all their land and women. That is, whatever women the Injuns leave for us!" He laughed obscenely, nudging Hanyost, and guffawing again.

Hanyost had worked on silently, ever more troubled. Clearly, his uncle Nicholas and everyone else in the valley would call him a traitor now, and indeed he called himself that. He went over and over in his mind the conversation between Brant and St. Leger after they had read Molly Brant's letter.

Deep in such thoughts, he did not hear his uncle speaking to him as they shared a simple lunch of bread and cheese. "I say, boy, you really are a dreamer, like they say."

"What?" said Hanyost.

"I was saying, just take a look at that raggedy quilt the rebels hoisted up over the fort. Looks like it's made out of pantaloons and bloomers."

Hanyost glanced over toward the fort and saw the same banner he had noticed that morning. A light breeze had lifted the flag and he could see that the blue square in the upper left corner carried a circle of stars. "It's not the same as the King's flag."

"It sure ain't!" observed Tenbrook.

"It's further proof of their treasonous intent," said Johan. "For all their fine protestations about how they shouldn't be taxed unless the colonies send some representatives way over to the parliament in London."

"What do the stars mean?" Hanyost tried to express some interest in the conversation.

"They say that's for the thirteen colonies," explained Johan. "But if that's so, why do they have thirteen stripes for the same thirteen colonies? Tell me that!"

"I don't know," said Hanyost.

"One of the smart ones deserted the fort yesterday," Johan went on. "He told us that the rebel leader Gansevoort claims this is the first time that the traitor's flag was ever flown in battle. Seems they heard that the parcel of thieves they call the Continental Congress came up with this new flag but Washington was too scared to fly it himself!"

"Back to work, lads." One of St. Leger's officers appeared around a bend in the trench.

117

"Yes sir, Lieutenant Bird, sir," replied Ten Brook with mock enthusiasm.

For the rest of the day Hanyost was silent, wrapped in his own thoughts, working beside his uncle and the other men until they were exhausted.

For all the long daylight hours laboring in the hot sun, Hanyost could not fully admit to himself what Molly's message had meant. But in the night, restlessly turning in his sleep on the hard ground, he had to face the reality that he had carried to St. Leger a warning that the militia was coming. Thanks to that warning, this huge army would be waiting for them. His family and neighbors would be slaughtered.

Finally, as the first grey light crept under the tent flap, Hanyost rose and went outside. His first thought was to run back eastward, to try and warn his Uncle Nicholas that their enemies had been alerted and were preparing an ambush.

He began to walk quickly toward the woods from which he had emerged the previous morning. If he had slipped past the lookouts once, he reasoned, he could certainly do it again.

"Halt!" Two men in green uniforms stepped in front of him. Their faces were familiar to him. He had often seen the burly red-bearded man with Alexander White, the sheriff of Tryon County before he fled to Canada with Sir John. The other was Henry Nellis, onetime companion of George Klock.

"Just stretching my legs," he answered. "Walking." He touched his shins. "My legs are stiff from digging the trench yesterday."

"Where have I seen you before?" asked the man with the red beard, suspiciously.

"I know him," said Nellis. "He's Hanyost Schuyler. He came in yesterday."

"Sure, I know who you are now," said the other man, smiling broadly and extending his hand. "You're the one who brought the message from Molly Brant. You deserve our thanks for letting us know that the traitors are coming."

"This here gentleman is Alec MacGregor," said Nellis. "He's one of them Highlanders Sir William brought over to be his personal bodyguard."

"Bodyguards?" laughed MacGregor. "Tenants is more like it."

"Not a bad lot, for all that they're Papists and like to wear skirts!" Nellis returned, as MacGregor took a humorous swipe at him with his huge fist.

"Pleased and proud to meet ye, lad," said the Scotsman. "Ignore anything said by this lamebrain to me left. Now, just get back to your regiment. You're likely to get yourself shot walking about for no reason."

21. Joseph Brant

As he returned to the tent, he found the other men emerging. "First, we'll have ourselves some breakfast," his uncle told him, "and then I'm going to let St. Leger know that we're not the sort to do the work of slaves for even one more day! I'm the one was in charge of his bateaux and if it weren't for me, he'd still be back in Oswego."

"Slaving away in the muck of that creek was not the kind of work I signed up for either," muttered Tenbrook, scratching himself and hitching up his woolen leggings.

"That's where you're wrong, Peter," said Johan throwing some salt pork into a frying pan. "That work needed to be done. When I volunteered to take charge of the boats, I suspected Gansevoort might have his boys block up Wood Creek with fallen timbers like he did."

"Where is Wood Creek?" asked Hanyost, wondering if there were another way he could escape from the camp.

"Let me explain," said his uncle. "We loaded up our bateaux at the King's fort in Oswego on Lake Ontario, and then we rowed up a couple of small rivers to Oneida Lake. Going was slow but we did all right until we came to Wood Creek, which goes from the lake nearly to the Mohawk River. That fort there is right at the portage between the creek and the river."

"And Gansevoort blocked up the creek?"

"He must have set a couple hundred men to cutting trees and tossing them in the creek, so we couldn't bring up our cannons for days. The savages and Butler's rangers did some skirmishing around the fort while I had charge of clearing out the creek. Took us days, it did, and we still haven't brought up the last two Cohorn mortars."

"Will the cannon knock down the fort?"

"The problem St. Leger has," Johan continued, "is that the fort is better built than he figured. The palisades are below the ground level of the glacis, which is what they call those sloping dirt embankments all around the fort. The cannons can't get a clear shot at the walls."

"Then his cannons are useless?"

"I would not say that, lad," returned Johan. "They can still point upwards and fire over the walls and land a ball or two in their midst. But we can't hit the walls and open up the fort to our attack, that much is true. And that is why St. Leger has us digging those damned trenches, so he can position the cannons for a direct shot against the walls."

"So, digging the trenches is the most important work we can do now."

"Here's some pork for you." Johan, frowning, handed him a tin plate. "Sorry we don't have eggs to go with it but we got some dry biscuit, if that'll suit you."

Hanyost munched on the fatty meat, wishing he had some venison. He saw Alec MacGregor approaching and felt a tremor of fear. Did he realize that Hanyost had been trying to escape through the woods?

"Morning, gentlemen," said MacGregor. "After you finish breakfast, get yourselves ready for a formation with Sir John."

"What's in the offing?" inquired Johan.

"He's mum on that for now, but I'll wager it has much to do with the news your brave nephew brought yesterday. You can be proud of that lad, Johan."

As the Scotsman strode off to the other tents, Johan said to Hanyost. "He's right, Hanyost. I am proud of you and most pleased that you've joined us loyal men and left that band of traitors behind."

Johan, Tenbrook and the other men began to pull on their green jackets and black leather regimental caps. "Sorry we don't have one of these outfits for you, Hanyost, but that doesn't mean you're not one of us, one of the King's Royal Regiment of New York."

Sir John assembled his men in formation. On the other side of the field, Hanyost saw other units gathering, Butler's rangers also in green, a small contingent of British soldiers in red, the Hessian mercenaries in blue.

"Line up straight and stand tall, lad," said his uncle as they took their place on a level field out of gunshot of the fort. "St. Leger has had a true military education in Great Britain and he insists on doing things proper, and Sir John is just the same. He's not like my fool brother, letting every man slouch about as he likes. These fellows know what discipline is, believe me!"

"Men, a decisive moment is upon us," Sir John began. "Thanks to the courage of one of your own, we have received word that the traitor Nicholas Herkimer is marching toward us with a large force."

The men looked one to another, some with a pang of fear but many with eager anticipation.

"General St. Leger is determined to maintain the siege and has placed a major responsibility on our regiment to do so. He is sending our native allies and Butler's Rangers out to meet and destroy the enemy. I will support their assault with a small contingent from our ranks. The majority of you will hold our positions here but remain in readiness to join that fight, if need be. Therefore, we will suspend work on the trenches today and tomorrow. Every man is to have his musket, powder and ball in readiness for any sortie from the fort. Artillerymen will keep up a steady cannonade throughout the day and night."

"That is all," Johnson concluded. "God save the King!"

"God save the King," the men echoed.

As Johan's unit readied their muskets, Henry Nellis joined them. "Johan, it seems that Brant has need of your gallant nephew."

"What need?" asked Hanyost.

"All he said to me was to get Hanyost Schuyler and have him report to me. And tell him to bring his bow and arrows."

"Why?" asked Hanyost.

"Around here we just follow orders. We don't ask why," snapped Nellis. "He said to bring a bow. That means he needs those who can use a bow and arrow, don't it?"

"Or maybe he figures you're half an Injun, and good at conniving up sneaking ways to fall on the militia," suggested Tenbrook. "Whilst me and your uncle miss all the fun."

"Joseph Brant is a genuine English gentleman, Hanyost, for all his red skin. If he says he needs you, then he has a sound military reason," Johan turned angrily on Tenbrook. "When he went to England he was received by the King himself and given every honor. He even translated the Lord's own Gospel of Mark into Mohawk."

"Prob'ly changed the words all around so's the Injuns could scalp us all and still go to heav'n."

Hanyost took his bow and quiver of arrows and shook his uncle's hand. "I will go to Joseph Brant, uncle."

Nellis accompanied Hanyost to the edge of a large circle of men gathered around Brant and an older, balding man in a green uniform

"Who's that old man in the green coat?" Hanyost whispered to Nellis.

"Don't you recognize John Butler? A few years back he was only Sir William's majordomo but now he's a regular colonel with his own regiment, all well-trained and disciplined men. Butler's Greens, he calls 'em. And that frisky pup on his right is his son Walter. He don't have his father's steadiness in my view."

"Brave soldiers," Brant spoke first in English, repeating more or less the same pronouncement in Mohawk. "The hour of battle is upon us. By this time tomorrow, the enemy will be ours!"

The Iroquois began to call out in their various dialects. They boasted of how many scalps they would take, of the mutilations they would inflict upon the bodies of their enemies. Hanyost shuddered, thinking of his Uncle Nicholas and all those neighbors who would be marching with him.

"We have received word, from a trusted source, that Nicholas Herkimer is leading his band of farmers right into our hands."

Brant then spoke in English. "Men, we have been given a chance to defeat the rebel army tomorrow as they approach the fort in an attempt to make us break off our siege. While you ready yourselves for the coming battle, Colonel Butler and I will take our lieutenants and a small force of picked men to scout the terrain and set up the ambush."

As Brant repeated his message in Mohawk, Hanyost heard him tell the Iroquois that they would take many scalps and that the Mohawks would burn the settlements in the Mohawk Valley and take back all their ancestral lands.

"Seneca, Cayuga and Onondaga brothers," he said, shifting to the slightly different dialects of those tribes, "you will take many women and children to replenish the longhouses of your tribes and many captives for torture."

Hanyost pictured his mother, alone in her small cabin as Brant and his followers descended upon her. How could she escape such horrors? How could he get away in time to warn his uncle of the deadly ambush into which he was leading the militia?

Butler then spoke directly to the Loyalists, thanking them for their courage and telling them that soon they would reclaim all the property that they had lost to "the traitorous rebels."

As Butler continued speaking, Hanyost glanced at his son. The younger man's eyes shone and he nodded with approval as Butler described the slaughter they would wreak upon the foolish rebels. What kind of men are these, Hanyost thought to himself, that they take joy in such bloodthirsty threats against their own people?

Finally Butler concluded, and his greencoated followers gave him a hearty cheer. Brant then called out several names in Mohawk, and he heard the old childhood name that Black Jacob had bestowed on him: "He-who-is-a-curious-bird."

Joining the Mohawks who gathered around Brant, Hanyost saw that each carried a bow. He saw Tekarihoga at Brant's side, evidently his chief lieutenant, and several other men whom he had known for years. "You are the warriors who will make it possible for us to destroy our enemies tomorrow. Come with me to the place where this will happen."

Both Butlers, with several of their men, joined Brant. When Sir John with three of his men and two officers in red coats arrived, they all set out for the surrounding woods.

JOSEPH BRANT

Portrait of Joseph Brant by Geo. Romney, 1776

22. Setting the Trap

The group moved quickly down the old military road into the surrounding forest. Great oaks, far larger than any still standing in the lower Mohawk Valley, towered overhead and cast a deep shade. The midsummer foliage was so thick a man could be only a few feet away and not be seen.

Brant was far in the lead, walking swiftly along the narrow, rutted road. Some of the French Canadians who had joined St. Leger's expedition were busy with axes, trying to widen the road. They paused, sweating and leaning on their axes as the men passed by.

By Brant's side were both Butlers, St. Leger's chief aide Lieutenant Bird, and Sir John Johnson. Their red and green uniforms contrasted with the lightly clad Iroquois, many of whom wore only a loincloth.

The larger part of the group was composed of Mohawks and Tories from Brant's own company. Hanyost, bringing up the rear in the hope of a chance to slip away, noticed that none of the Senecas were represented, and he thought this strange since they appeared to form the single largest contingent at Fort Stanwix.

The day grew oppressively hot and humid. The mosquitoes and biting flies were merciless. A lumbering black bear went crashing into the deeper woods, startled by the rapidly moving body of men.

In the distance Hanyost could hear the occasional boom of one of St. Leger's small cannons and reports of single musket shots. Those left around the fort were evidently making good on the order to keep up the pressure on Gansevoort and the several hundred Americans trapped with him inside the fort.

As they passed a clearing about a mile into the woods, several of the men grabbed quick handfuls of blackberries. One of the Mohawks made a joking remark to Tekarihoga, who had been walking beside Hanyost.

He did not fully understand the more vulgar expressions of the Mohawks, but he was always ready to expand his knowledge of the language.

"What is it they say?" he asked Tekarihoga.

"They make a joke about the red haired ones," the Mohawk answered, wiping blackberry juice from his chin. "This is where I killed two red-haired girls who came from the fort to pick berries nine days ago. Their scalps are drying in my tent."

The other Mohawk repeated the joke and both men laughed. Hanyost recoiled in horror as he saw the ripped shreds of a calico dress caught in the berry bushes.

He hurried ahead to join the others, ever more eager to escape and warn the approaching militia.

After several miles, the country became hillier but the pace did not slacken. All of the men, like Hanyost, were accustomed to long days traveling by foot.

Around midday they halted on a forested ridge and gathered around Brant.

"This is the place," he announced, first in Mohawk and then in English, "where we will kill the rebels and take many scalps."

Looking down from the ridge through the thick foliage, Hanyost could make out, forty feet below, a small stream, surrounded by marsh, and a log bridge that carried the road further eastward.

"Our scouts bring us word that Herkimer camped last night near old Fort Schuyler, then forded the river and is now moving slowly this way. Very slowly."

The Mohawks laughed, and one called out, "They march like squaws carrying old men on their shoulders."

Brant joined in the laughter. "They are farmers and are not fond of walking in the woods. They like to walk only as far as the barn to milk their cows."

The Mohawks laughed again. "We will soon be pulling their udders!" called out another Mohawk.

"Our scouts report that there are already many stragglers, and some sit down on tree trunks to rub their sore feet!"

When the laughter subsided, Brant continued, "But we must not be overconfident. They will rest and will eat well tonight, probably near Oriska, the village of their friends, the Oneidas. They will only have to march six miles to this ravine, as far we came today from the fort. They may be farmers but there are many of them. At least eight hundred left Fort Dayton yesterday and Gansevoort has about seven hundred soldiers inside the fort. If they both come out to make battle, we will be trapped between their two armies. And do not forget that many of our Seneca and Onondaga brothers have only tomahawks and spears."

The Mohawks looked anxiously, one to another. Hanyost knew that the Iroquois did not relish open battle, preferring stealthy ambushes, and were always distressed to lose even one of their own warriors. Each warrior was heedless of his own life in battle but the tribe, he knew, sorrowed greatly for any one of them who was killed.

"This is why the trap in which we shall catch Herkimer must be perfectly made."

Taking a stick, Brant brushed away pine needles and scratched a rough map on the forest floor. "This line is the road and this is the stream. Here is the bridge over which they must cross. This is the only way they can bring their wagons and cannon up to the fort. They must come through the ravine that lies below us, cross the bridge, and begin to climb the sloping road up to where we are now."

The Mohawks and Tories listened closely. Hanyost could see quickly how the plan would work, and how vulnerable the militia would be.

"We will be spread out along this ridge," Brant continued, "and on the opposite, lower ridge. There is much swamp on that side and no way for them to escape our attack, so fewer men will be needed there. Sir John, I suggest that you command that ridge."

"Gladly," said Sir John. "We will be closer on that side and able to fire volley after volley into their ranks and then advance with bayonets, driving them back against their own baggage train."

"Here," Brant pointed to one end of his rough map, "is where we are now. I will ask Old Smoke and Cornplanter to position their Seneca warriors here, to block any further advance of the rebels."

"Why are there no Senecas with us now?"

Brant was not pleased by Hanyost's question.

"They need more talk among themselves but they will be here. I will also place some of my own company here above the bridge."

"Colonel Butler, with your approval, I suggest that your men be mixed with the Senecas along the high ridge to the south. My brothers the Senecas have many inexperienced young warriors and need steady men beside them. They greatly respect you and will be honored to fight by your side."

"We too will be honored to fight beside your Seneca brothers," said Butler.

The Mohawk chief pointed to the far end of the narrow valley on his map. "Once the rebel army is fully within the ravine, I will lead the majority of my men in closing the trap behind them. Then they will be completely surrounded."

"Then we will kill them all, "said Walter Butler, his eyes shining with excitement.

"But there are several dangers that could be our undoing."

"What dangers?" asked Hanyost, wanting to know the weaknesses in the plan, if only to preserve some hope that his uncle and neighbors could escape destruction.

"First is that their line of march will be so strung out by their own laziness that they will not all have entered the trap by the time we want to spring it. But there is nothing we can do about this. We cannot send them a message to stay together so that we can kill them more easily."

The younger Butler laughed out loud at this.

"So, however many, and we must hope that it will be all of them, are in the trap, we must spring it when the leading men begin to climb up out of the ravine. My scouts tell me that Herkimer is in the front, riding a white horse, so that when we kill him many will flee and my warriors can run them down and scalp them one by one."

"My men, too, carry scalping knives," grinned Walter Butler.

"There is a second danger." Brant paused and continued. "Even though our scouts tell us that Herkimer is advancing without sending out any scouts on his flanks, that may change as he nears the fort. Particularly if the false-hearted Oneidas from Oriska join him as they have threatened to do. If Oneidas or even his white scouts flank out in these woods before he brings his army into the ravine, then he will uncover our trap and stay out of it. This is why I have brought my best bowmen here to spend the night watching for any men Herkimer may send out."

"The final danger to this plan is that one of us will be too eager to kill and shoot before my signal and then the rebels will be warned before we can fully strike them. This is a great danger that we must prevent."

Brant lifted a brass whistle from a rawhide strap around his neck. "This is an English sergeant's whistle, given to me by your father, Sir John. When I see that the entire rebel force is within the trap I will blow the whistle. Thus."

The Mohawk held the whistle to his lips and blew a resounding blast. "This can be heard throughout the ravine. No one must fire until they hear this whistle."

"Now, may I suggest that each of the commanders and aides take a close look at your assigned positions, scouting the terrain and vantage points. Then meet again here in an hour to see if the plan meets with all of your approval."

Brant spoke in Mohawk to his closest followers, the ones who carried bows. "Stay here with me. You also, Hanyost Schuyler."

23. Ataentsic Returns
The night of August 5-6, 1777

Hanyost counted twelve warriors remaining as the others fanned out to reconnoiter the ravine.

Brant placed his hand on Hanyost's shoulder.

"Hanyost Schuyler, Butler and Johnson tell me that you are not a man that I should trust." Brant looked into his eyes. "Your heart is in two places, this I know. Your family also is split in two."

Hanyost said nothing. He returned Brant's gaze without wavering.

"Yet my heart tells me that I can trust you. The one called Black Jacob, who was very wise, told me that when you grew, you would become a man who would one day save my life. I believed him then and I believe him now. He knew that you are not like other white men, that your soul is that of a Mohawk."

Hanyost still said nothing.

"Your skill with the bow excels most Iroquois warriors of this age, who have learned to rely on the white man's muskets and steel hatchets. I will need your skill and your flint-tipped arrows tonight and tomorrow. And I truly believe that my own life may depend upon that skill."

"If I can prevent it, I will not let you die tomorrow," said Hanyost with complete honesty.

"These other twelve also excel most other warriors with the bow."

Brant motioned for the twelve to form a semicircle around him. "Each of you will stay here in the woods until tomorrow to watch for flanking scouts that Herkimer or the Oneidas may send out tonight in advance of their army. If you see them, you must kill silently. Even the tomahawk allows a man to scream out in agony. Only arrows must be used. Arrows straight to the heart."

"You are men of Connajoharry. All of you know Hanyost. He is one of you."

Hanyost could see that the other warriors, except for Tekarihoga, accepted him. He saw suspicion in his eyes and looked away.

"You heard Hanyost ask why no Senecas are here with us, and I will tell you the truth. The Senecas are hesitating to join in this battle. Yet they have the largest numbers here. John Butler and I will go back to talk further with them. If they agree to join us, we will attack the rebels. If they do not, I will lead all of the Mohawk warriors away from this place. But now I ask Tekarihoga to be your chief and to assign you the places from which you will watch today and tonight."

"We are ready to kill silently," said Tekarihoga, stringing his bow and beginning to descend the hillside toward the narrow, meandering creek. Hanyost was horrified every time he thought of what this man, whom he had known and liked for years, had done to the red-haired girls.

Wanting to conceal the repulsion that he felt, he walked by Tekarihoga's side. As they passed below the ridge, he saw Brant watching them. Then the thick forest enveloped them in its wet darkness as they waded across the marsh.

As they moved quietly along, Tekarihoga silently indicated points where each scout should position himself. Soon, the thirteen were spread out in a line spanning all possible approaches to the ravine.

Each man was invisible to the others, able to communicate with the warrior on either side only by mimicking the calls of the redbird and the yellowbird. One call for warning and one to signal that no enemy had been seen. At nightfall they would change to the call of the owl, once that all was well and twice for an approaching enemy.

Hanyost was to the south of the road, covering the center of the swamp. He slowly moved through his assigned area, searching for places where a determined enemy could find a foothold to cross over the swamp. He found only one spot where the ground was firm enough and the underbrush sufficiently thin to allow an enemy scout to pass.

Lying on a small hillock screened by cattails and purple loosestrife, Hanyost spent the afternoon watching and waiting. Stray deer passed and a wary fox. Every hour or so, particular bird calls sounded, letting him know that the scout to his right and to his left had seen no enemies. Tempted to doze, he fought off sleepiness, waiting for night when he planned to slip away toward the American camp. He rehearsed in his mind many variations of how he would convince his uncle of the danger that he faced.

As evening came, the last of the redwinged blackbirds returned to their nests in the marsh and hungry bats emerged, flying rapidly among the tall hemlock and oak. Hanyost ate some pemmican from his pouch and drank a little water from the muddy stream.

Clouds obscured the rising moon and the darkness became nearly impenetrable to his eyes. Then he heard a branch break, and the rustle of leaves. Someone was approaching. Hanyost slid forward on his stomach.

The clouds parted for a moment and in a shaft of moonlight he could see three white men. He recognized Adam Helmer, known as a swift runner throughout the valley. "It's slow going, lads, but we can't risk the road. They're sure to have posted lookouts there. "

"If we go this slow, we'll not get to Gansevoort in time to tell him to sally out and attack the English and Injuns from the rear," said the second man. Hanyost recognized the voice of Hannes Demuth. His old captain!

"Nor for him to sound the signal gun so's Old Nick and the boys can attack 'em straight on," said the third man.

"Quiet, lads, or we'll be roast dinner for the Mohawks," warned Helmer. "Now, follow me, slowly."

Hanyost thought quickly. If the three men followed this route, they would pass directly by him and once over the ridge, would have a fair chance of reaching the fort. He considered speaking to them, but decided not to risk it. "My uncle has already branded me a traitor, and they might simply kill me here," he told himself. "Then what good would I be to anyone?"

He watched the three as they moved out of the marsh only feet from where he lay concealed, and proceeded up the slope toward drier ground. Helmer seemed capable, he thought, and they should make it to the fort. What Brant dreaded, that St. Leger's army would be caught between two large American forces, might come to pass. Hanyost feared the slaughter of his friends among the Mohawks but, thinking of the two red-haired scalps, he could not hope for anything other than a victory by the militia.

Hours passed, and the other Mohawk scouts continued to signal that no enemy had been seen. He was ready to move through the swamp and begin a quick run toward Herkimer's camp. Then Hanyost heard a very faint movement less than ten feet away. Who could manage to come so close unnoticed? No animal would move so quietly. Straining his eyes in the darkness, Hanyost notched an arrow and pulled his bowstring partly back.

"Would you take my life?" asked a gentle voice. Her hand was on his arm, pushing aside the arrow. "Have you so soon forgotten your promises to me?"

"Ataentsic!"

"Quietly, quietly." She put her fingertips on his lips.

"How did you…"

Keeping her fingertips on his lips, Ataentsic sat beside him on the leafy ground. "I will whisper and you will whisper back."

Hanyost marveled at the closeness of her. In the darkness only the barest outline of her face was visible but her voice and her touch awakened all his old feelings.

"I was out gathering herbs in the forest, along the shores of Lake Oneida," she whispered. "When I returned to the camp, my friends told me of your arrival. Thayendenegea said that you would be here. So, I have come to you."

"How did you find me in this darkness?"

"The forest spirits guide my eyes and my ears."

"Do you know that a great slaughter is planned for this place tomorrow morning?"

"I know this."

"Can it be stopped?"

"I am only a childless and manless woman, Hanyost." He was startled at her use of his name.

Years before, their speech followed the prescribed Mohawk etiquette yet now she was as direct as any white man, and more than any white woman.

"I know nothing of the wars in which men bring wounds and death to each other."

"It is not safe for you to be here."

"The danger will not come until the sun rises," she said, taking his hand and placing it upon her breast. "We have a few hours still to be together in the darkness."

24. The Oak Tree
August 6, 1777 early morning

Hanyost awoke with a start. Where had Ataentsic gone? He parted the cattails and peered into the marsh. A grey pre-dawn light filtered down through the thick stands of hemlock and white pine. Squirrels were busy, running noisily along branches and through dry leaves on the hillside. Had he imagined, or dreamed, that she was here? Or was she a ghost or forest spirit?

He cautiously rose from the hillock, bow in hand, an arrow ready. He gave the call of the redbird. No response. Then he saw Ataentsic, bending down to drink from the stream. He gazed at her until she turned and looked back at him, smiling.

"You have changed since we were children together in Connajoharry," he said to her.

"How could I not?" she returned.

"You do not follow all of the old ways."

"The ways that I follow now," she said, "are older than the ways of the people who live in the longhouses. I follow the ways of the First Mothers, from the days before men learned to take each other's scalps."

"There will be much dying today," said Hanyost. "Come away with me. We can go south or west, away from this war."

"I must stay, Hanyost. There will be many wounds that will need healing."

"You are a healer but I am not. There is nothing I can do here."

"You are not a killer of men, this I know of you."

"What is there in a battle for one who is neither a killer nor a healer?"

"Then you will go away?"

"Not alone."

"Then you will stay." Ataentsic brushed his lips with her own. "You will know what you must do on this terrible day."

Swiftly running up the slope, she vanished into the thick woods.

As he lost sight of her, he heard the redbird's call from a Mohawk. Still no sign of Herkimer's scouts. This was the time, and past time, for him to seek out the militia and warn them of the impending ambush. Hanyost moved back down the hillside and began to wade into the shallow marsh water, holding his bow high.

"Where are you going?" He heard Tekarihoga's voice behind him. Turning his head, his bow still high, he saw that the warrior's bow was taut, an arrow pointing at Hanyost's heart.

"I thought I heard someone in the shallow water."

"Why did you not give the bird-signal?"

"I could not be sure."

"Thayendenegea wants to see you," said the Mohawk, suspicion evident in his voice. "Go. Walk in front of me."

Hanyost climbed up the slope and soon found Brant where they had met on the previous day. Now, however, the ridge was filled with men. At least two hundred Seneca warriors, armed with a mix of muskets, bows and spears, were fanning out along the ridge line. Sir John was leading a portion of his Royal Yorkers down the hillside toward the other side of the ravine.

Brant's Tory followers were in buckskins and covered in their own version of Iroquois war paint. Some were even stripped down to loin cloths, as were most of the Mohawk warriors.

"Hanyost," Brant said quickly. "I want you on the highest place so that you can see where I am fighting this day. This ridge is high, that oak is even higher. Climb up and conceal yourself. Keep your bow ready to kill any man who is about to take my life. Understand?"

Without a word, Hanyost, reached for the lower branches of the tree and hoisted himself upward. The tree was an ancient one, perhaps a hundred feet high and at least eight feet around. Not sure if he called to God the Father or to the tree itself, Hanyost prayed as he moved upward from branch to branch: You, who have lived many lives of men, find some way for me to save men from dying today.

He continued climbing until finally the trunk and branches thinned out too much for him to go any higher. Lodging himself in the crook of two strong branches, concealed completely by the oak's broad leaves, he looked out to where the battle would take place.

The old military road sloped downward, from a rise about a half mile to his east. On the marshy bottom the land leveled, dense with sumac and other quick-growing plants, but free of taller trees. From his height, Hanyost could make out the places along the ridge where the Iroquois and Tories were crouching in the thick woods.

Looking downward, Hanyost could see the massed warriors of the Seneca, Cayuga and

Onondaga nations. They seemed unable to maintain silence and were in a high state of excitement.

St. Leger himself in his brilliant red coat was conferring with what appeared to be two Seneca chiefs. Then, surrounded by his officers, he moved back out of sight.

Hours passed and still the militia did not appear.

Watching carefully, Hanyost detected moving leaves that revealed the location of Johnson's Tory regiment on the opposite side of the ravine. He wondered if his Uncle Johan was there, ready to kill his own brother and neighbors.

Then, in the small clearing on the rise to the east, Hanyost saw two men appear. They paused on the high ground and seemed to peer into the surrounding forest. A few minutes later, several other men, also on foot, joined them.

Then Hanyost saw the magnificent white horse that identified his Uncle Nicholas. He will be the target of every musket with that horse, muttered Hanyost to himself. How can I warn him?

He judged the distance to be half a mile and calculated that he had a chance of sending an arrow that far, although he had never done so before. The militiamen would see an Indian arrow falling from who knows where and would be immediately alerted to the danger they were in!

Quickly choosing the lightest arrow in his quiver, Hanyost looked downward to make sure that the Iroquois below did not see him. He pulled the bowstring to its limit and aiming very high, he let go. The arrow soared in a great arc above the trees, scarcely visible against the overcast sky, and came down just in front of the small group of men.

No one reacted.

The fools! Why won't they see it? He realized that he had only heavier arrows, suitable for deer and bear, left in his quiver. Although he feared it would not go even so far as the first, he chose another arrow, pulled back, and let fly.

He watched the arching arrow soar high against the sky and then fall, too short, into the marsh.

Again, no one reacted. Perhaps the Iroquois or Tories had seen the arrows? But even if one of them had, would he know from where the arrow had been shot?

Several other men, also on horseback, now joined General Herkimer at the far end of the narrow valley. By their gestures, it was evident that they were talking. Hanyost could catch snatches of their words, obviously loud and heated, to carry so far. What can they be arguing about?

The argument, for such it clearly was, continued as several more men on foot appeared, surrounding the General's horse and gesturing wildly. What are they shouting about, Hanyost kept asking himself. Do they understand the danger they are in?

Then Hanyost heard his uncle's angry, shouted words, carried by the wind: "March on!"

The distinct sounds of a cheer from many men rose up above the trees.

Now, he understood why the officers were arguing. His uncle had been waiting for the cannon to fire, the agreed-upon signal that that Gansevoort was ready to coordinate his attack with Herkimer's. Somehow, the others had succeeded in convincing his uncle to advance into this death trap!

But why would my uncle give such an order? Hanyost asked himself. Can't he see that this is a perfect place for an ambush?

"LEAD US ON!"

Depiction of Herkimer arguing with his officers before Oriskany, from *The Mohawk Valley During the Revolution* by Harold Frederic, 1877

25. The Ambush
August 6, 1777, from mid-morning to noon

The long line of the Tryon County Militia was advancing slowly down the hill into the ravine. At its head were the two men who had first appeared, accompanied by half a dozen others. They seemed to be Indians and, and as they reached the log bridge, Hanyost recognized the Oneida Thomas Spencer and his brother. Thomas' father was white and Hanyost had seen him frequently, trading at German Flatts. He looked for signs of other Oneida scouts in the woods on either side of the column, but even from this height, none were visible.

Then came the General astride his white horse. Behind him marched two abreast the men of the valley. There was his uncle by marriage, Aunt Delia's husband Peter Bellinger, also mounted and leading a large body of men, most of whom were familiar to Hanyost. He saw Abel Hunt sauntering along with his friends, and there were the seven Snell brothers from across the river and many more familiar faces. His Shoemaker cousins were laughing as they walked, looking as if they were out for a morning's hunt.

Casting his eyes along the line of marching men, he could see that they were growing fatigued as the already warm and humid morning became even warmer. Gaps appeared in the line, slowing up those who came behind. Then he saw the lumbering oxcarts moving down into the ravine. He realized that a good portion of the militia had still not entered the trap. There was still time to save them from destruction!

Hanyost reached for his quiver, intending to send another warning arrow, which maybe this time would work. As he turned to better position himself, his quiver upended and the arrows fell downwards, through the leaves and branches.

The Senecas below would see him! But no, they had disappeared from beneath the tree and were already creeping closer to the edge of the roadway. Hanyost began to quickly descend the great oak, branch to branch, nearly losing his grip in his haste to reach the ground. Finally, he was able to drop down lightly onto the forest floor. No one was in sight. Looking in the underbrush he found first one and then four more arrows.

The flint points had broken off three. Still, the blunted arrows would serve well enough to send a warning. Holding the arrows in his right hand and the bow in his left, he cautiously looked about for an opening in the dense foliage.

Moving silently, he found that the Senecas had crept downhill to the very edge of the woods. Breaking with Brant's orders, they had lost the advantage of the higher ground. Those with muskets were aiming at the first few militiamen who were already midway to the bridge.

If only I can warn them, he thought to himself, they will have a chance! But how? Where can I find a clear space to shoot an arrow?

Frustrated by his inability to get past the hidden Senecas, he hurried back as quickly as he could and began climbing up the huge oak. From that height he would find a clear space in the foliage for his arrow.

By the time he reached midway up the ancient tree, Hanyost could see that the forward unit had started to move more quickly, leaving a wide gap between Herkimer's group and Peter Bellinger's company. He let fly a blunt arrow, directly over the treetops beneath which the Seneca waited. It landed between the two units of the militia.

He let fly a second, directly at his uncle, but in his anxiety he aimed too low and the arrow fell uselessly into the shallow creek.

He reached for a third arrow.

But what were those fools doing? Men from Bellinger's company ran forward toward the creek, throwing down their muskets. They fell onto the mossy banks of the creek, dunking their heads and scooping up handfuls of water.

A single musket shot rang out!

Then came the roar of many muskets and the shrieking war cry of the Iroquois.

Herkimer wheeled his white horse at the sound of gunfire to his rear. The two Spencer brothers fell dead as they ran back from the bridge toward the gunfire. Iroquois warriors came shrieking out onto the roadway, tomahawking two of the Snell brothers at the bridge before they could raise their muskets.

The fire was continuous now, one long roar of thunder. Militiamen were falling all along the line of march. A Seneca warrior rammed his spear into Jim Seeber and then turned to kill his uncle Rudolph as he ran to his aid. An officer from one of the companies galloped forward and fell suddenly from his horse. Bellinger had dismounted and was trying to form his men into a circle on the exposed road, as fire poured onto them from both sides of the ravine.

Hanyost could see Brant's mixed Tories and Mohawks falling upon the heavily laden carts, killing the oxen and blocking any retreat. He recognized his uncle's slave Sam as one of the drivers, using his whip to drive back the Mohawks. Brant's war cry echoed across the narrow valley. Hanyost saw him lift up a scalp and wave it in triumph.

Within moments, the entire line of marching soldiers had dissolved. Some were running for the rear, only to come up against the overturned oxcarts. Mohawks fired from behind the carts, cutting down many. As they ran out to take scalps, several were shot down in turn by militiamen who were moving off the road into the cover of the woods. Gunfire and screams of agony sounded from the dark forest as ambushers and ambushed clashed hand to hand.

Then he saw Herkimer's horse crumple, blood splashing its white flank. His uncle tumbled to the ground, barely avoiding being crushed by the falling horse. He tried to stand, only to collapse, his leggings red with blood. Two men grabbed his arms to pull him back from a pair of Iroquois with raised tomahawks. Both warriors fell dead, hit by fire from the remaining Snell brothers.

He saw more warriors cut down by musketfire from the circle formed by Bellinger's already badly depleted company. More Iroquois came pouring down from both sides of the ravine. Herkimer was shouting something as the two men carried him behind a stand of hickory. Hanyost could hear nothing but the shrieks and the gunfire. Black gunsmoke drifted across the ravine.

The fighting was everywhere across the level bottomland of the ravine as men struggled hand to hand, swinging muskets like clubs. A tall Indian on horseback, a scabbard dangling from his waist, swept back and forth across the roadway, slashing at Senecas and Mohawks. No one seemed able to stand against him until a musket ball shattered his wrist. Leaping down from the horse, the Oneida was quickly joined by a woman and a younger man – his wife and son? Together the three of them took cover behind a pair of fallen oxen and stood off twenty warriors, the wife reloading pistols and muskets and handing them to her husband and son as they kept up a steady fire.

Transfixed by the horrible spectacle, Hanyost hung forward on the branches of the oak. I could have stopped this, he kept saying aloud. I could have stopped this. Why didn't I go to the militia last night? Why did I wait until it was too late to warn them? I am the one who brought Molly Brant's letter here. I am the one to blame for this massacre!

Hours passed as Hanyost clung to the branches, paralyzed by remorse, unable to act, telling himself over and over that it was too late, too late.

The skies grew darker as the fighting continued. Bodies filled the creek and piled up along the bridge, and others lay face down in the open marsh.

The militiamen stood behind trees and fired from their protection. Hanyost saw that when a puff of smoke revealed a shooter's location, a warrior would run to that tree and tomahawk the man before he could reload.

Then came a crack of thunder, louder than all the muskets, and a tremendous flash of lightning. Sudden torrents of rain poured down and slowly the musket fire sputtered out, as the flintlocks became too damp to fire. But this was a summer storm, born of the great heat, and would soon pass.

An idea came to him.

He had two good arrows left. The fighters on both sides would seek cover in this storm and visibility would be greatly reduced as long as the downpour continued. If I follow the ridge eastward, I will reach the spot where Joseph Brant is waiting out the storm. He trusts me. He will want me by his side because of the prophecy. With one arrow I will kill him. Then his men will kill me. But with their leader dead, they will not continue the fighting.

The rain came down even harder as Hanyost dropped to the ground and began to jog quickly along the ridge, slipping several times in the wet leaves. He heard a few shouts as militiamen or Tories saw him flash by, but he knew that, for now, their muskets were useless.

He soon he reached the second small ravine where Brant's men had ambushed the baggage train. Advancing more cautiously, bow in hand and arrow notched, he was still forty yards back from the road. Moving even more cautiously, he crept to the edge of the woods where he expected Brant's men to be sheltering from the rain, which was now beginning to slacken.

Then he heard a piercing scream and pushed aside the screen of leaves.

Brant and his men were walking among the fallen settlers and warriors who lay scattered amid the upended carts and dead oxen. They were looking for men who were still alive.

Tekarihoga was pulling a spear from the man who had just screamed. Blood spurted into the air.

Beside him a ragged-bearded Tory, his mock warpaint washed off, lifted a bloody scalp and uttered his poor imitation of a war cry.

Brant stood tall among them, pointing out another man who was still alive. "That one has much life in him," he said. "Take him as a captive."

Edging closer, Hanyost drew back his bow and held it steady on Brant. At this distance he could send the arrow straight into his back.

He held the bowstring taut, hesitating to release it. He had never killed a human being.

Just then, one of the Indian bodies moved. A man, his face smeared with blood and mud but somehow familiar, rose up on one elbow. Brant and his men were facing away from him.

The Indian managed to rise to his feet. He had a tomahawk in his right hand. He staggered slightly, and moved toward Brant. He raised the tomahawk over Brant's head.

Hanyost released the bowstring.

His arrow flew straight.

His arrow pierced the man's right arm.

With a scream he dropped the tomahawk.

In the same instant Brant spun around and drove his own tomahawk into the man's face, splitting his skull. The man fell, blood and brains splashing out.

Brant saw Hanyost at the forest's edge, his bow in his hand.

"The prophecy is fulfilled," Brant cried out in triumph. "The white man with the heart of a Mohawk has saved my life."

In a daze, Hanyost walked forward, Brant's Tories and Mohawks all around him.

"You have saved the life of Thayendenegea," said Tekarihoga, embracing him. His face was spattered with fresh blood. "I will not doubt you again."

Brant, too, embraced him. He then thrust his own bloodied tomahawk into Hanyost's belt. "This day you become a Mohawk warrior."

"This dog fought with the Oneidas," he said, kicking the dead body. "They are no longer our brothers."

Hanyost looked down at the dead man. Even with his face split in half, Hanyost recognized Dadawat.

Herkimer at the Battle of Oriskany.

Herkimer at the Battle of Oriskany.

From the Picture Collection of the New York Public Library

26. After the Thunderstorm
August 6, 1777 midafternoon

The thunderstorm ceased as suddenly as it had begun.

"Herkimer has been seen on the western hillside," Joseph Brant told his men. "He cannot walk but still he directs the battle. He has gathered what remains of his men in a great defensive circle on the hillside. They have their leader now and will not be so easy to frighten. He is very calm and leans against a tree smoking his pipe."

"I know where I'd like to stick that pipe!" yelled one of the Tories. "Then we'll see what a big man old Nick Herkimer is!"

"We have not defeated them yet," Brant warned. "A messenger has brought word that St. Leger is sending fresh men to join Johnson and they will attack from the west. We will circle around and attack them from behind. In this way we will finish off the rebels."

Brant selected three men to guard about a dozen terrified prisoners. They included Sam and another slave of Herkimer's. After making sure that all of the captives were thoroughly bound, Brant led his main force into the woods on the other side of the road. They found a few more wounded men in the woods and killed them with spears and bayonets.

Hanyost walked numbly beside them. He saw Abel Hunt lying on his back in the shallow water of the marsh, making a terrible gasping sound as he struggled to breathe. Blood bubbled on his chest. His eyes seemed fixed on Hanyost. At that moment one of the Tories drove a bayonet into the man's throat.

"Friend of yours?" laughed the Tory, seeing the look on Hanyost's face.

"I knew him," he managed to say.

They moved onward, slowly climbing uphill where there was no path, stepping over fallen trees and around huge boulders.

"Spread out in a half-moon," Brant told his followers as they reached the top of a ridge and moved toward the heavily wooded hillside where he believed Herkimer to be.

"Move slowly, slowly. We will not strike until we hear the fusillade from Johnson's guns."

Hanyost found himself on the far tip of the advancing crescent, near the bottom of the slope and closest to the road. In his quiver was one arrow. His only other weapon was the bloodied tomahawk that Brant had given him.

He moved forward out of the crescent, crossing through the woods below Herkimer's position, unsure where or why he was going. Just knowing that he wanted to be away from all the killing. The image of Ataentsic came to him and he imagined finding her, going with her far away to the west where there was no war.

The scattered sound of musket fire had resumed, very close by.

Hanyost saw a Seneca fall, the top of his head shot off. A puff of black smoke appeared behind a tall hemlock. Another Seneca ran toward the tree, long spear in hand. A second man stepped from behind the hemlock, took careful aim, and shot him through the neck.

Yet another Seneca ran forward and another man stepped out and coolly shot him down. Two men behind each tree, thought Hanyost. One will reload while the other fires.

Creeping farther down the hill on his hands and knees, he saw the same tactic repeated with equal success. Two more Senecas lay dead.

Then, coming directly at him through the trees he saw a line of men. They cannot be the soldiers Joseph Brant is waiting for, Hanyost thought. They have no hats and they are wearing buckskin, like the militia.

But no! One man's coat brushed a branch and he saw a flash of green cloth. They are Johnson's Royal Greens. They have turned their coats around to deceive the militia.

He heard a cheer from just behind him.

"Hurrah!" called out a voice. "Vischer's men have come back! Now we're all here! We'll give these villains a beating now!"

"This way!" called out another voice. "Come and join the fight, boys!'

Hanyost could see that Johnson's men would be directly upon the militia's lines before they opened fire. The slaughter would be terrible.

He recognized the man in the lead as Alec MacGregor, who had stopped him the day before when he tried to leave the camp.

Reaching for his one remaining arrow, Hanyost let fly without hesitation.

The arrow flew straight through the web of low-lying branches toward the red-bearded Scotsman, who was waving in a friendly way at the militiamen. Several came out from behind their trees to join in the general cheer.

The arrow caught the highlander's coat and pinned it back against a tree. MacGregor fumbled to close his coat, ripping it away from the tree. But too late. The green coat was revealed for all to see.

"It's a trick, boys!" he heard his uncle's voice cry out. "Open fire! Open fire for all you're worth."

A thunderous barrage ripped into the advancing men. Blood spurted on the buff coats.

The survivors of the first blast tried to stand and return fire just as another murderous fusillade struck them.

Militiamen rushed forward from the trees, smashing skulls with their muskets, fighting hand to hand with fists and knives.

Hanyost saw Jacob Gardinier, a farmer from German Flatts, rush forward with a short spear, which he jammed into MacGregor's stomach. He knocked aside the musket of a second man and stabbed him repeatedly.

"Hold your lines!" His uncle's voice rang out again. "Hold your lines! Officers! Get your men back to the line."

Pulling back, the militiamen left piles of bodies on the slope.

Hanyost saw Sir John Johnson, his face red with rage. "Cowards!" he screamed. "Stand and fight!"

Then the ones who were still alive ran, stumbling over fallen timbers and scrambling to their feet as scattered shots dropped them by ones and twos.

Hanyost turned and ran in the opposite direction, just in time to see Brant raising his arm for the signal to attack.

"Stop! Stop!" he shouted. "Johnson's men are all killed. You have to pull back!"

"What are you saying?" Brant held up his hand in the signal to pause.

"Johnson's men turned their coats inside out," Hanyost panted. "They were almost into the militia's lines but then they saw that their coats were green. The militia killed most of them and the rest ran."

"It is true," said Tekarihoga, who had just joined them. "From the top of the hill, I could see Johnson's men running back up the road. Johnson cannot stop them."

"This battle is over," said Brant. "Come, let us go. Give the call for retreat."

"Oonah! Oonah!" the Mohawks cried as they fell back, deeper into the forest.

27. The Clearing in the Forest
August 6, 1777, evening

The British encampment was a scene of nearly complete destruction.

As Brant's band emerged from the surrounding woods, they saw plumes of smoke rising from their burned tents and supplies. More than twenty of those left behind to keep up the siege lay dead amid the debris.

"Look," said Hanyost, pointing to the fort, where three British ensigns flew below the red, white and blue banner of the rebels. "Have we captured the fort?"

"T'aint likely," said Peter Tenbrook, who was picking through the remains of a smashed ammunition wagon. "The rebels came out whilst you were away fighting Herkimer and gave us a beating. Took our flags and now they fly 'em lower than their own, by way of showing who's on top now."

"Plundered the whole camp, they did," Ten Brook shook his head in dismay. "Then they sent for wagons to haul the loot back into the fort. Muskets and powder, kettles, blankets, anything they could steal."

"But what of St. Leger?" demanded Brant. "He left the ravine to come back and keep the rebels from sallying out of the fort. He said he couldn't trust Lieutenant Bird with that responsibility. Did he do nothing?"

"Oh, the general took prompt action," snorted Tenbrook. "He pulled his precious redcoats back to protect the artillery and didn't lose a single piece.

Just my good luck I was out of the trenches heeding nature's call, you might say, when Willett and his rascals came charging out at us. First, they sounded three big cannon blasts and then they opened the gate and came at us."

"Too bad about your uncle," Tenbrook added offhandedly to Hanyost.

"He is dead?"

"No, but the rebels grabbed him and three others who was in the trenches and carried 'em back to the fort. Sir Johnny told him he didn't have to go ambush Herkimer since it was his own brother they planned to kill. Johan says, thanks sir, and now, look what's come of it."

Thinking only of Ataentsic, Hanyost walked away from Brant and Tenbrook, searching the broken faces of the dead. The first two were British regulars, their blood a darker red on their once bright coats. Near them, on a slight hill, lay three of the blue-coated Hessians, mercenaries hired by the King. These five must have stood and fought, he realized. Beyond them lay more bodies, face down in the mud and grass, shot in the back as they ran for their lives.

At the edge of the Mohawk camp he found what he was dreading. An Iroquois woman was lying near the smoldering remains of a tent. Her black braids were matted with dried blood. In her hand she still clasped a healer's rattle. Hanyost's heart seemed to stop. Ataentsic?

He knelt beside the body, placing his hand gently on the shoulder, stroking the bloody hair. Then he saw another woman's legs beneath the partly burned remains of a wagon. He rose unsteadily to his feet.

The second woman was also dead, the back of her skull caved in.

Neither was Ataentsic.

Then he saw her, walking out of the acrid, drifting smoke, carrying a tightly wrapped infant. The frightful angle of the tiny head told him that the child was dead.

"Ataentsic."

She stiffened as he wrapped his arms around her. All around him rose howls of grief and rage from the returning Iroquois warriors, but he heard only her soft moaning.

Together they fashioned a litter to drag the bodies of the dead women and the infant into the forest. Coming to a windblown clearing deep in the woods, they spent hours digging a common grave. Ataentsic broke evergreen branches and made a blanket to cover the three.

After they filled in the grave, they carried round stones from a stream bed, piling them up to protect the lost ones from wild animals.

All the while, Ataentsic did not speak.

Hanyost held her as they sat together beside the mound of earth. A light rain pattered through the leaves and darkness filled the forest. The sky became clear and moonlight filtered down through the tangled canopy of branches.

Both were exhausted but neither slept.

In the moonlight, a fox entered the clearing and sniffed at the mound.

Hours passed.

While it was still dark, the first few bird calls signaled the approach of dawn.

Ataentsic broke the long silence.

"These two were my sisters-by-other-mothers. It is from them that I learned to become a healer."

"They became a family to you."

"When I went away from Connajoharry, I left my clan and my people. I had no one. I wandered for many days in the forest. I thought many times of throwing myself off a cliff or into a lake. I did not want to live."

"Then they found me," she continued after a long pause. "They taught me of the old ways of the world. Of the ways that women followed in the days before tribes came to be, when families lived alone in the forest, far from other people. They taught me to know the healing herbs and the names of the small spirits of the forest who aid human beings in distress. These names have long been forgotten by those who live in longhouses."

Hanyost waited for her to continue.

"They were women without a tribe or a clan, as I was. When we came to a village, whether of the Iroquois or other tribes, the people honored us as healers."

"I wish we could have given them a more suitable funeral," said Hanyost, thinking of the solemn church service held for his grandfather Herkimer, who had died two years earlier. "I wish we had someone to say words over them as we placed them in the earth."

"This is the way they would wish," Ataentsic answered him. "This is the old way that they taught me. As soon as the spirit leaves the body, we return it to the earth in a place like this, deep in the forest that is the source of all living things. No words are needed."

"Many died yesterday," said Hanyost. "But these women should not have died. They were not warriors."

"When the men came from the fort, they killed everyone as they ran. My sisters did not run. They had no fear of death."

"You were there when the soldiers came from the fort?"

"I was on the far side of the camp in the healing lodge," she answered, her voice empty of emotion. "I could not leave the sick ones. The men from the fort did not come there."

"Ataentsic." He took her hand. "This is not our fight. We are not on either side. Again, I ask you to go away with me."

The sky began to lighten and the morning bird song filled the woods.

"I cannot do any good things here," he told her. "Whichever choice I make, more die."

She was silent, watching yellow birds dart from branch to branch.

"Before you came to me in the forest, I saw three messengers from my uncle going to the fort. I listened to them speak. I let them pass by. If I had not let them continue on their way, the men would not have come out of the fort and killed your sisters and the infant."

"I must go back, for there is good that I can do. There are many wounded and I have been too long away."

Then she stood up and began to walk back toward the fort.

"Ataentsic," he implored her. "Stay here with me."

"You know that I cannot."

"Then I will return with you." He took her hand. "I can be of help to you with the wounded."

They walked together until they came back to the cleared area where St. Leger's forces had made their camp.

Portrait of Sir John Johnson by John Singleton Copley

28. Blood Lust
August 7, 1777

Ataentsic was talking with an old Cayuga woman carrying a large basket crammed with broken and half-burnt belongings. As the two spoke in low voices, the old woman kept casting evil looks in Hanyost's direction.

He turned away and found himself staring at Alec MacGregor's mangled body as it was carried past by two of Sir John's Royal Yorkers. A third walked behind, carrying a shovel. Hanyost looked about, wondering if anyone had seen the arrow he had sent into the highlander's coat a day earlier.

Ataentsic clasped the Cayuga woman's hand and rejoined Hanyost. "I will go to the camp of my people now," she told him.

"I will come with you."

"You will be safer if you stay here with the whites."

"The Mohawks know me as a friend."

"They are angry now. They will see only your white skin."

"But they believe that I saved Joseph Brant's life," He was resolved not to be parted from Ataentsic again. "They will not be angry at me."

"Listen to me, "she said. "They are torturing and killing the white prisoners. The English general is angry about this. He has commanded that the torture and killing stop. My people refuse to listen to him. If this dispute over the captives cannot be settled, there may be fighting between your people and my people."

"I will stay here, but if something bad happens, promise me that you will go to the forest place where we buried your sisters. I will meet you there."

"Yes," she said hurriedly. "I must go."

Hanyost watched her and the old Cayuga woman disappear beyond the hillside. When they were gone, he remained standing where he was, uncertain of what to do next. He wondered what had happened to his uncle Nicholas and the rebels who had survived the ambush. He did not think it likely that they would attack the camp. Too many men from the valley lay dead in the ravine.

He heard the faint sounds of a fiddle from the fort. Are they celebrating, he wondered. Do they not know of all the killing in the ravine? He wondered why the sortie from the fort had taken the rebels only as far as the camp. He could not understand why they had not pressed on to Oriskany to save his uncle and his neighbors.

Hanyost knew there was no longer any reason for him to find the militia now, and he also knew there was no reason for him to stay here, except for Ataentsic. Having seen his Mohawk friends killing the wounded, he could no longer tell himself that he was one of them. He thought about what Ataentsic told him of the Iroquois torturing prisoners.

He did not think that the Americans in the fort would hurt his uncle Johan. But maybe they would. Having seen such horrors and death at Oriskany, he no longer knew what anyone might do.

"Come here, you!" He saw Walter Butler walking toward him from the direction of the large tent. "Yes, you, Schuyler! Come over here, damn you!"

Hanyost noticed that Butler's leggings and military jacket were spattered by blood. He had clearly done his share of killing.

"They say you speak and understand the language of the Six Nations, is that right?"

"I speak the language of the Mohawk."

"How about the other tribes?"

"The languages are similar. I can understand some of what the others say."

"That'll do," said Butler. "We're meeting with the big sachems now and Brant is doing all the translating. My father talks good Injun but he's sick and my other translators got themselves killed yesterday. I want to have a white man who knows the lingo, just to keep Brant honest."

Passing through a line of Hessians, they entered the general's tent. St. Leger, his face red, was arguing a point to Brant, who listened impassively, his arms folded. Two Seneca chiefs, whom Hanyost recognized from Oriskany, glared at St. Leger. Several other Cayuga and Onondaga leaders stood behind the Senecas with equally hostile expressions on their faces.

The whites were grouped behind St. Leger and Sir John Johnson, who was seated beside the general. Hanyost recognized Lieutenant Bird as well as several officers from Butler's and Johnson's companies.

Brant said a few words to the Iroquois before answering St. Leger.

"I also deplore the acts of savagery which my fellow countrymen have inflicted upon the prisoners. I recognize that such actions are contrary to the rules of war."

"I am gratified to hear this, Captain Brant," said St. Leger. "But despite your personal view of the matter, your people have already killed a great many prisoners. I have reports that some of the prisoners have even been eaten! We are the King's army, Captain Brant, not a band of cannibals!"

"My people are very angry," said Brant. "Many brave men were killed yesterday. Many chiefs and honored warriors are dead. My people's anger must be appeased."

"Your people have no cause for such anger," argued St. Leger. "These deaths are the inevitable losses of war. Herkimer and his men suffered a far greater number slain and wounded."

"And the screaming!" said Sir John. "I could hear them all the way over on this side of the camp. I can understand that some of the braves want to take vengeance but must they do such fiendish tortures on the poor wretches? It really is too much to ask us to countenance, as Englishmen."

Brant turned to the Iroquois and spoke with them for several moments while the whites looked on. Hanyost listened intently. The other chiefs were arguing that they should depart immediately for the Mohawk Valley and proceed to slaughter all the women and children they could find.

"I too would like nothing better than to roast their infants on the point of my spear," he told them in their own language, "but we are few in number and if the whites join together against us, the Six Nations will be destroyed forever."

"My brothers are still very angry," he then told the whites. "They wish to go now and attack all the unprotected settlements of the Mohawk Valley. In this way they will take vengeance on the families of those who killed their warriors."

"That would be desertion! They have agreed to remain here and maintain the siege!" St. Leger practically shouted. The other Iroquois murmured in alarm, touching their tomahawks. Butler grasped the hilt of his sword.

"Perhaps there is a way that we can resolve this impasse, to everyone's advantage," Brant said.

"Yes?" Johnson sounded skeptical.

"We could send messengers to the fort with a flag of truce. You could tell Gansevoort and Willet the simple truth, that you are having difficulties restraining the Iroquois from laying waste to the valley, and implore them to surrender as the only way to keep the warriors under control."

"That's not a bad idea," said Butler. "And if they needed further persuading, we could tell them that if we have to storm the fort, the Indians can have all of them for dinner!"

As the general mulled over Brant's proposal, Sir John added, "I agree that we should use the threat of an Indian massacre to terrify the garrison, but certainly, as civilized people, we must limit the number of captives who are killed. I would insist that our native allies turn over to us however many captives are still alive."

"Good suggestion, Sir John" said St. Leger. "But I would modify it."

"In what manner?" asked Johnson.

"I would suggest to Captain Brant that he tell his people they can keep, say, a dozen captives, and do their worst on them tonight. That ought to satisfy their blood lust. Then, tomorrow we'll hoist up a flag of truce and have our chat with the rebels."

Brant explained the proposal to the Iroquois leaders. After about an hour of discussion in Iroquois, they reluctantly agreed to the twelve captives. As the sachems passed out of the tent, still arguing, Brant did not even notice the presence of Hanyost.

28. Officers of the King

"We cannot permit the Indians to just walk away from the siege," said St. Leger as soon as the Iroquois were out of earshot.

"No, we could not maintain the siege without them, that's certain. We will only have about four hundred white men left if the savages go," agreed Sir John. "But hopefully we can persuade Gansevoort to surrender once he realizes how hopeless his position is."

"Is it really that hopeless for the rebels?" asked Walter Butler. "They're warm and snug and have plenty of provisions while we are huddled out here with scarcely half a dozen tents for over twelve hundred men. Last night most of my rangers had barely enough blankets left to rig up any kind of covering against the rain."

"The natives are in a nasty mood, there's no gainsaying that," said Lieutenant Bird. "They lost not only their tents but most of their clothing and food. The Senecas are complaining that they even lost their sacred medicine bundles in Willett's raid, and that affects them deeply."

"Well, if the rebels can be made to understand our difficulties in controlling the wrath of the savages, they may well be terrified into surrendering," said the general.

"That prospect, sir, could rebound to our disadvantage," Sir John warned. "If the rebels become overly frightened, they'll be even more unwilling to open the gates to us. They'll fear, and with good reason, that the Iroquois will slaughter them all."

"We can make that point very clear in our letter to Gansevoort," said St. Leger. "I will personally inform him that this will be his last chance to surrender without a general massacre of everyone inside the fort."

"But why won't they just decide to hold out as long as their supplies last?" asked Butler.

"Despite his youth," said Sir John. "Lieutenant Butler may have a valid point. "The rebels have a large force on the Hudson under Philip Schuyler's command. I am sure that Gansevoort is hoping for Burgoyne's defeat, which would then allow the rebels to send another relief expedition here."

"Oh, he's a fool if he believes that," scoffed St. Leger. "Didn't Burgoyne conquer the impregnable fortress at Ticonderoga? He will have no difficulty sweeping aside Schuyler's rabble and taking Albany. General Howe will march up the Hudson and join him there, as planned, I am sure."

"I wouldn't wager my last shilling on Burgoyne, General, if I were you," said Butler. "My father's men have many contacts among the settlers from here all the way to the Hudson and they tell me that Burgoyne is bogged down in the woods. He has his men cutting a road before them all the way from Lake George down the upper Hudson valley."

"Nonsense, Butler!" exclaimed St. Leger. "I'll agree that General Burgoyne moves cautiously but you can't discount the brilliance of his taking Ticonderoga. Abercrombie lost hundreds of men there against Montcalm and still couldn't achieve his objective."

"And that farmer Ethan Allen with a few Vermont ruffians took it in a single night and without a shot, didn't he? Found the commander in his night shirt is what I hear."

"But the fortress was not seriously defended at that point!"

"I hear it wasn't all that well defended this time either. My men tell me that there were only a handful of rebels manning the walls when Burgoyne arrived with his six thousand professional soldiers."

St. Leger was nonplussed. "In any event, we can't fight General Burgoyne's battles for him. Our orders are to take this fort, by one means or another, and I certainly feel that it is worth the effort to make one final argument for surrender to the rebels. If they refuse, our cannons will soon be in place to blast them all to hell. "

"I agree with that strategy," said Sir John.

"I too, agree, despite my doubts as to the rebels' response," said Butler. "With your approval, I will go the Indian camp and find some likely officers among the captives whom we could persuade to add their voices to ours." He paused, before adding, "If the savages left anyone worthwhile alive, that is."

He motioned for Hanyost to accompany him and left the commander's tent.

Once they were outside, Butler asked him. "Was Brant telling the truth about what the other Indians were saying?"

"Yes, they wanted to go down the valley and kill everyone they could find."

"And do you think they'll be satisfied with twelve captives?"

"I do not know."

"But you grew up with these savages, they tell me. Do you know how long they usually practice their cruelties before they are satisfied?"

"I have not seen them like this." Hanyost answered honestly. "I know them in times of peace. I do not know them in times of war."

"But you do understand what they are saying, don't you?"

"Yes, I can even understand most of what the other tribes are saying." Hanyost added an example: "The Senecas told him that they came only to see the fighting. They did not intend to join in the battle yesterday and were angry that Brant shamed them into fighting, especially since they lost so many chiefs. They were angry at Brant and I do not think that he can control them very much longer."

"Good," Walter Butler clapped him on the shoulder. "That's the kind of thing I need to know."

Butler called together a dozen of his rangers. As the group of armed men walked toward the forest side of the siege lines where the Iroquois were encamped, Butler said to Hanyost, "Now, when we enter their camp, I want you to listen close to the Indians as I talk to their leaders. We plan to deprive them of some of their choice captives and I want to know if any of the brutes seems ready to attack us."

"I will listen."

"And since you say you've never seen these savages at their most vicious, be certain not to let it show if you are shocked by the cruelties you will witness."

30. Three Captives

Walter Butler was right. Hanyost was horrified by what he saw as they entered the Iroquois encampment. A blackened corpse hung from a framework of branches. One of the legs was missing. A group of white men, completely naked, was huddled together within a ring of screaming Iroquois, who were poking at them with spears and knives. Their pale bodies were badly bruised and covered with blood.

"Looks like the savages are getting ready to run the poor wretches through the gantlet again," observed Butler. "They never get tired of that game."

"Where's Brant?" asked one of his men.

"He is there," said Hanyost, trying to control his trembling voice. "Talking with two of the Senecas who were in St. Leger's tent."

"That's Cornplanter and Old Smoke," said Butler. "Big chiefs among their people. Hanyost, go tell Brant we want to talk with him. The rest of you, keep your muskets ready but don't take aim at the savages just yet."

Hanyost walked unsteadily across the open space, feeling the eyes of the Iroquois on him. He was very much aware that there were hundreds of Indians and only a handful of Butler's men.

Suddenly one of the warriors broke away from the circle around the captives and came running straight at him.

Hanyost kept walking forward at a steady pace, watching the fast approaching Indian from the corner of his eye.

"Hanyost Schuyler!" Brant saw him coming just as the Indian raised his tomahawk. Hanyost dropped as the tomahawk swung and grabbed the man's arm, wrenching it back and throwing the warrior to the ground.

Other warriors cried out and came running toward him.

"This man is our friend!" Brant shouted to the angry warrior, who had risen to his feet in a rage. "This man has saved my life!"

The Indians backed off, glowering and muttering. The smell of rum was strong on them.

"Why did you come here?"

"I have come with Walter Butler," Hanyost took a deep breath. "He's over there. He wants to talk."

"Now?"

"Yes."

Gathering his closest Mohawk followers, Brant walked over to Butler's group. The shrieks of the naked men grew louder as their tormentors began to toss flaming brands on their exposed skin.

"Ugly business," said Butler.

"I grant you that it is."

"St. Leger wants you to give us a couple officers we can use to make a case to Gansevoort that he should surrender the fort."

"It will be dangerous to take away any captives now. The Senecas want their revenge. My own people, too."

"It's the general's orders."

"Who do you want?"

"I don't rightly know. Which ones are officers?"

They looked toward the naked men. Beyond them a few black captives huddled, still dressed in tattered garments, and evidently not subjected to torture. Hanyost recognized Sam and another of Herkimer's slaves.

"Not any of the black ones," laughed Butler. "Though they seem to be in better condition than the whites."

"Those are mine. I will need slaves for after the war when I live in Nicholas Herkimer's big house."

Hanyost couldn't believe when even this last reason for siding with Brant was taken away. Didn't he claim that he respected their old Tuscarora friend? And now to make slaves of his people?

Hanyost wished that he had sent his arrow into Brant's back yesterday when he had the chance. Now, as he thought about it, he was no longer sure if he had meant to hit Dadawat or Brant when he released the arrow.

"Which whites do you want?" Brant asked. "I certainly cannot give you all of them."

"The General said that your boys could have a dozen to torment," Butler reminded him. "There must be thirty right there, and I don't know how many you killed last night."

"Pick three of them now. I'll try to save whoever's left by morning and bring them to you."

The battered men all looked the same to Walter Butler. "Hanyost, you know these people. Who would you choose?"

He looked closely at the pitiful men, their eyes filled with terror. "I see John Frey. He became the sheriff of Tryon County after Alexander White went to Canada. He is an officer. And Frederick Bellinger, I think he is a colonel. He is not as important as my uncle Peter Bellinger but he is an important man."

"And the third?"

"I know Richard Wollover from Fort Herkimer."

"I will tell them that the General needs those three men, and that he will give us presents if we make a gift of those men to him. It will take some talking but I think this can be done."

Hanyost waited anxiously with Butler and his men as Joseph Brant talked, first with the Seneca chiefs and then with the men who encircled the captives. Voices were raised and then subsided. Finally Brant led the three men, still naked and bound together by the neck, to Butler.

"Now go, and go quickly," he said. "Before they change their minds and kill all of you."

Frederick Bellinger recognized Hanyost as they all began to jog back toward the white side of the siege camp. "I see you sided up with your Tory uncle," he managed to say through broken teeth.

Hanyost said nothing.

Once the captives were unbound and clothed in some cast-off rags, Butler brought them to St. Leger's tent. By now, he had come to regard Hanyost as one of his own company and he made sure that he stayed close.

"Good work, Butler," said St. Leger. Turning to the captives, whose arms remained bound behind their backs, he told them, "You men know that Herkimer's militia was smashed yesterday. My reports tell me that he had barely a hundred men still standing at day's end, and now they're creeping back home like whipped dogs. The ravine is full of dead bodies. And we lost only a handful, a few savages and one or two whites."

The captives fixed their eyes on him, not knowing what would come next.

"Thanks to me, your lives have been spared. And I will continue to protect you and send you home to your families if you help me to end all this madness."

"And we also have received word that General Burgoyne has defeated Schuyler and is now in Albany," Sir John lied. "So don't count on any help from that quarter."

"Our desire is to save the lives of the seven hundred men, women and children in the fort," continued St. Leger, "and to keep the savages from going down the Mohawk Valley and killing everyone they find."

"General Schuyler is defeated?" asked Bellinger.

"And a prisoner of Burgoyne," added Johnson.

"We are prepared to make a final offer to Colonel Gansevoort," St. Leger explained. "If he surrenders the fort now, we will spare the lives of all within. If he refuses, I cannot control what will happen. If we have to reduce the fort by artillery, as I intend to, the savages will surely massacre everyone. And then they will storm through the valley, killing your women and children."

He paused, to let the message sink in. "I want you men to write a letter to Gansevoort telling him that the war is lost and that he must surrender to us. This is the honorable course of action, as officers, for you to take, so that no further lives are lost in vain. Do you agree?"

"I will not be a traitor," said Bellinger, eyeing Hanyost. "Unlike some."

"Nor will I, " said Frey.

"Nor I," Wollover added weakly.

"I see," said Sir John. "Very bravely said. Now tell me your ranks."

"I am Lieutenant Colonel Frederick Bellinger of the German Flatts Company of the Tryon County militia.

"And I am Major John Frey of the Palatine Company."

"I'm Private Richard Wollover, from Fort Herkimer, sir."

"Private?" said Sir John. "We need only officers for this letter."

Taking out his pistol, he held it to Wollover's head. "Since we do not need privates for this purpose, I will shoot this man if you, Colonel Bellinger, and you, Major Frey, will not do your duty."

"We are not traitors!" said Bellinger.

"Very well." Johnson cocked his pistol, checked the priming, and locked his eyes on Frey and Bellinger. "Are you certain?"

Then he hauled the man to his feet and took him outside. A moment later the blast of a pistol rocked the tent. Johnson came back to the now badly shaken remaining captives.

"We truly need only a colonel," he said, calmly reloading his pistol. "We can dispense with a mere major like Mr. Frey." He lifted Frey to his feet and prepared to take him outside.

"No, no," cried Bellinger. "We'll sign the letter. Just tell us what to write."

"Good," said St. Leger, turning to Lieutenant Bird. "Bring us paper and ink, please."

Aghast at what he had seen, Hanyost stumbled outside with Walter Butler. A few yards away, he saw two Royal Yorkers standing over Wollover, tightly bound and with a gag stopping up his mouth.

"You see, Hanyost, even you believed the ruse," smiled Butler. "Sir John's a clever fellow, isn't he? Of course, this private really is of no use to us. We will send him back to the savages."

31. The Ultimatum Rejected
August 8-9, 1777

Walter Butler was not happy when his father
rose from his sick bed the next day and was placed
in charge of delivering the ultimatum to
Gansevoort. "I should be with him," he complained
to Hanyost. "I know how those rebels think. I
studied law with the best of them, you know."

"Law?" asked Hanyost, who had found a flint
outcropping and was busy chipping himself some
new arrowheads.

"Yes, my young savage friend," laughed Butler.
"And not the mish mash of traditions your Mohawk
brothers keep talking about. I studied the King's
law in Albany and, were it not for this blasted war,
I'd be making myself quite wealthy by now."

"Perhaps your father wished to keep you out of
danger?" offered Hanyost.

"Exactly so! He thinks I am still a child and
wants to protect me. He said that Gansevoort might
well seize our ambassadors and hold them in
exchange for the captives."

"Do you think Gansevoort will agree to
surrender?" Hanyost asked.

"No, he will not, but mark my words, he will
bargain for more time to consider the offer, as he
did with the first offer Lieutenant Bird made him
when we arrived here. Gansevoort still thinks that
relief is coming."

"Is he right?"

"He might be," Butler speculated. "Johnson was
lying, of course, when he said that Burgoyne had
defeated Schuyler. Our spies tell us that Burgoyne

is running low on provisions. He may have to retreat back to Canada."

"Then Schuyler could send men here to fight us."

"Yes," agreed Butler. "This is why we have to take this fort, and soon, by one means or another."

"General St. Leger believes that he can destroy the fort with his cannon."

"Hanyost, you're a clever fellow yourself, for all that your neighbors thought you a fool. You've hit the very heart of the matter. The artillery!"

"The artillery?"

"Yes, the artillery." Butler lowered his voice. "You see, St. Leger was on the St. Lawrence when he heard that Burgoyne had taken Ticonderoga. He feared that all the glory would be Burgoyne's so he hurried on without waiting for strong enough ordnance. The ones he has here are what you call light artillery and mortars. They are not sufficient to reduce the fort. The savages told him that the fort was a strong one but he disregarded them and preferred to believe that the fort was still in the sorry state it was two years ago. The fool!"

Hanyost continued chipping away at his piece of flint, wondering once again at the great partiality shown to him by Walter Butler. He suspected that Butler valued him because it was he who had selected Hanyost, while the rest of the rangers had all been chosen by his father and answered, ultimately, to him and not to Walter.

Later that afternoon, John Butler returned from Fort Stanwix. Just as Walter had predicted, Gansevoort was stalling for time. After listening to John Butler and reading the letter from Bellinger and Frey, he asked that St. Leger's terms be put into writing. When St. Leger agreed to do so, and that document was delivered to the fort, Gansevoort pled for additional time to consider the offer with his chief officers. In the meantime, both sides agreed to what Gansevoort called "a cessation of arms."

The next morning John Butler was furious.

"I told you this would happen," his son told him.

"The insolence of this puppy Gansevoort!" the elder Butler exploded. "He feigns to listen to our offer, buying himself two days without a shot fired, and then he sends us the most insulting answer."

"What did he write?" asked his son.

"Let me recite it for you verbatim," said the father, sputtering with rage. "It is my determined resolution, the impudent fellow says, with the forces under my command to defend this fort and garrison in favor of the United States to the last extremity."

"United States!" laughed the son. "United Rascals is more like it."

"What will happen now?" asked Hanyost, who was continually at Walter's side now.

"Just listen, you young whelp of savagery!" snarled the father, cupping a hand to his ear.

A moment later, all the cannons roared.

"Now they will discover what it means to mock the King's power," said John Butler. "St. Leger has vowed to annihilate them to the last man!"

32. The Lodge of Healing
August 10-12, 1777

The bombardment continued without interruption for the next four days. St. Leger placed his soldiers around the fort with instructions to shoot at any rebel foolish enough to lift his head above the parapet. With the trenches nearly completed, he brought up the mortars and positioned them to fire horizontally against the fort.

Despite this barrage, by night as well as day, the fort remained in American hands, and its red, white and blue banner still fluttered defiantly over the bastion. Return fire from the fort's cannons was rare and no more effective than that of the besieging force. Sharpshooters in the fort, however, had better luck and succeeded in killing or wounding a number of men.

The Iroquois remained a problem for St. Leger. Each day Hanyost watched as sullen chiefs filed into the general's tent and emerged many hours later, looking no happier. He glimpsed Brant from a distance twice, with other chiefs, but saw no sign of Ataentsic.

Finally, he confided in Walter Butler that he had a woman friend in the Mohawk camp and he wished to visit her. "You young scamp!" said Walter. "It's quiet lads like yourself that have all the women. Go and see your doxie, but be cautious. I wouldn't want to see you scalped and flayed by those savages. I may have further need of your skills."

Circling far out along Wood Creek, he approached the forest camp of the Indians as cautiously as Butler had recommended. Climbing a tall tree, he scanned the area and saw little activity. He wondered if some of the tribesmen had already deserted the siege.

Then he saw the scattered barrels and guessed that St. Leger had been buying time with his allies through plentiful gifts of rum. They must still be sleeping off the effects of the strong drink, he surmised, deciding to risk a closer look. There were few enough tents left but where were the places for the sick and wounded? It was there, if anywhere, that he would find Ataentsic.

Along the edge of the camp at the farthest point from the marshes, he found a hastily constructed longhouse of the ancient kind. Peering through a space in the bark outer covering of the structure, he saw Ataentsic, sitting beside a moaning warrior. He quietly entered the lodge and sat on the ground beside her.

She touched his hand without ceasing her murmuring chant to the dying man, for such he surely was. Hanyost saw that a deep wound on his chest had begun to fester and turn greenish black. A fierce heat came from the man's body and his eyes were clouded.

As they crouched beside him, the warrior began to twist and turn in great discomfort. His breathing grew harsher and louder. Ataentsic bent over him, placing her lips on his ear and whispering words that Hanyost could not hear. Then, with one final breath the man became still. Ataentsic remained with him, still murmuring until the man's hands became cool.

"I will summon his clan so that they may take him," she said. "Now, go and wait for me in the place where my sisters have gone back to the earth."

Two hours later, as the sun neared its zenith, she came to him in the forest.

As the sun grew low many hours later, he said to her, "I have a plan for peace that I will bring to Walter Butler. In this way I will do good instead of evil."

"What is the plan?"

" I will tell Walter Butler that he and I should go down the valley and meet with people in their homes and tell them that there must be peace, that too many have died already. If the people want peace and tell the leaders, there will be no more war."

Ataentsic smiled. "You are like the small boy with whom I played in Connajoharry."

"Why do you say that?" Hanyost was hurt. Was she mocking his plan?

"I must do something," he insisted. "I have done much harm bringing the war to this place. I know the people on both sides. They will listen to me now. They will listen to Walter Butler. He knows their laws."

"But Hanyost," she pulled him gently to her. "The whites are fools. They have ever been fools. They will not listen to you now."

"I have done too much that is wrong," he tried to explain his feelings to her. "If I had not brought Molly Brant's letter, there would have been no ambush in the ravine. If I had not shot an arrow into the man's green coat, the King's men would not have been killed. I am not on either side. I am on both sides. This is why people will listen to me."

"Hanyost, they will not listen to you. They will put a rope around your neck and hang you."

"But what else can I do? You will not go far away with me, will you?"

"You know that I cannot."

"Then I will go with Walter Butler and make the people listen."

"Hanyost, you know that this is child's talk. Why do you think the people would listen? There has been too much blood. People are too angry."

"Black Jacob said I would do a great deed for both our peoples," Hanyost insisted. "He knew many things."

"He was a very old man," she said. "Old men are sometimes as foolish as small boys."

"And sometimes the small and the old are wiser than those who are in the summer of their days."

"Sometimes," said Ataentsic. "Sometimes."

33. Walter Butler's Plan
August 13, 1777

While the bombardment of Fort Stanwix
continued, with little effect, Walter Butler and
Hanyost had occasion to spend much time together.
Eager to become his father's equal in
communicating with their Indian allies, Walter
insisted that Hanyost teach him Mohawk.

The lessons began at breakfast and continued
through the day as they and the other rangers
manned their posts facing the fort. For appearance's
sake, Hanyost held a musket but never used it,
keeping his head low as balls whistled past.

When he tired of the effort to memorize the
unfamiliar vocabulary and grammar, Walter would
regale Hanyost with tales of his voyage to London
the previous winter with Joseph Brant, Guy Johnson
and the rebel prisoner, Ethan Allen.

" Captain Brant and I met the king himself, but I
confess that it was Joseph who most attracted his
majesty's interest. They spent quite a bit of time
chatting and his majesty was well pleased with
Joseph's undying loyalty to the crown."

Hanyost listened with interest, asking a question
now and then to better imagine that far-off world.
When Walter described the great military reviews
and the naval shipyards, Hanyost was puzzled.

"If the King has so many soldiers, why did he
not send more to this fight?"

"What?" Walter, caught up in his own story, did
not always relish interruptions.

"There are over a thousand red men here and not
so many whites, and most of the whites are from

our country. Why did the King send so few redcoats?"

"Don't forget the Hessians," Walter reminded him. "They are formidable soldiers."

"Yes, but you told me that King George had to pay another king to send them here."

"Hanyost, you're a likely lad, but some of these matters really are beyond your understanding." Walter returned to gazing along his gunsight at the tops of the distant palisade, hoping that a rebel might stick up his head.

This was the same answer the white men in the Mohawk Valley gave him when he asked about the world outside the valley. What had Klock said about such matters not being for blacks or fools like me?

Later, as they finished a final Mohawk lesson for the day, this one on the words for various weapons, Hanyost brought up the idea that had been simmering in his head for some days.

"Lieutenant Butler, I have a plan I want to tell you."

"A plan?" Walter smiled. "A plan to visit your tawny sweetheart perhaps?"

"No, this is a plan for talking to the people in the Mohawk Valley."

"What are you saying? You want to go home? They'll skin you alive if you do."

"No, my plan is this," Hanyost burst out into the longest speech he had ever made to Butler. "You and I go to talk to the people in the Mohawk Valley who have not been in the war. We will tell them they should make peace. They should not fight any more. We will tell them that the King will forgive them if they do not fight any more. We will tell them about all the people killed in Oriskany ravine.

We will tell them there must be no more killing. They will listen to us. They will listen to you because you are a lawyer. They will listen to me because I...I ..."

"Because you've fought on both sides?" Walter laughed out loud. "I can't imagine that distinction will win you many friends!"

Hanyost paced nervously back and forth. He had little experience expressing his ideas to others and now he felt that he had garbled everything.

"I know many people who do not want to be in this war," he added. He thought of John Shoemaker, whose brother was married to his Aunt Delia. His cousins had told him that their father and their uncle had quarreled over the rebellion and stopped speaking to each other.

Walter stroked his chin. "You do sound a bit daft when you say it all at once like that but you may have a good idea. You're saying that we should meet with settlers who are either loyalists or who would be happy to join us if they knew how badly Herkimer was beaten. Meet with them and sway them to our side."

"Yes..." he answered uncertainly. What Walter Butler said seemed to be what Hanyost meant. "But I ..."

"Of course, I understand," said Walter. "You can't put the idea into just the words you want, but I see what you're saying. "We know that Herkimer had only 150 men left to fight by day's end. This means that his militia is shattered as a fighting force. Meanwhile, we are doing nothing here and Herkimer can claim he has won a great victory. But if we show up with even a small contingent and rouse the loyalists and those who are wavering, we could swing the whole region to our side. Then it won't matter what happens to this damned fort. Gansevoort can stay inside and rot and we'll already be in Albany. We might even beat Burgoyne to Albany, imagine that!"

Hanyost saw that Walter was taking his idea in directions he had not intended, but he couldn't find the words to stop him.

"Hanyost," Walter said. "You are absolutely right to point out that I am a lawyer. And I'm a damned persuasive one, too, if I do say so myself. Now, you just sit yourself down. I'm going to see my father right now and let him know what I plan to do."

Hanyost sat on the ground outside Walter Butler's tent as the sun went down behind the fort. He saw the red, white and blue banner being lowered and heard the sound of a bugler from within the walls.

Several hours later he found himself suddenly shaken awake.

"Good news, Hanyost!" Walter Butler was exultant. "It took some hard persuading on my part but St. Leger and Sir John have agreed to support my plan. They will put me in command of about a dozen rangers and some Mohawks. We set out tomorrow before first light."

"You talked to your father?" Hanyost was still half-asleep.

"Oh, Papa was reluctant at first. He wanted to shield me from any danger, as always. Of course there's risk in a venture of this sort, I told him, but if we succeed, we can turn the enemy's flank, fall on Schuyler from behind, and practically end this whole rebellion."

"I thought…" Hanyost began. "I thought that just you and I would go to talk with the people."

"Just the two of us?" Walter smiled, and not for the first time, at his companion's naiveté. "I agree that the force should be small and travel fast but two men? That's not going to impress anyone, nor allow us to defend ourselves. Now, go finish your sleep. We'll be up in a few hours."

34. Flag of Truce
August 14-15, 1777

The smell of death was overwhelming.

Dawn was filtering through the trees as Walter Butler's band paused at the edge of Oriskany ravine. A wolf howled in the distance, then another. No one wanted to move.

"Onward," said Walter. "This is the quickest route."

When not one of the over twenty Mohawks and Rangers moved, Walter Butler angrily stepped forward and led the way down the sloping road that marked the farthest point Herkimer had reached. They marched over the log bridge where the two Spencer brothers fell, their footsteps loud on the rough-hewn wood.

As they reached the bottom of the ravine where most of the killing had taken place, their pace faltered. Bodies lay across the road, mangled beyond recognition by the forest animals.

They all heard the wolf before they saw it, a huge grey monster ripping away at a corpse. Pulling a single flint-tipped arrow from his quiver, Hanyost took quick aim and let fly. The beast made a horrifying snarl as the arrow struck home. It staggered toward them, its fangs bared. The men backed off, raising their muskets.

The wolf dropped to its forelegs.

"What in hell are you doing?" screamed Butler.

Hanyost stepped forward and drew from his belt the tomahawk Brant had given him. He swung back and smashed the animal's skull.

"Didn't I order you to maintain silence?" Butler kept screaming. "We have no time to waste killing animals.

Hanyost said nothing and kept walking. Peter Ten Book and the other Tories looked strangely at him. One of the Mohawks praised his skill. "In the days of our fathers, we too could kill a wolf with a single arrow."

"We will name you Wolf-killer," said another.

For the rest of that morning, Hanyost marched with the Mohawks. For a time, as he had in his childhood, he felt completely at home with them.

Leaving the old military road well before they reached more settled areas, the men forded the Mohawk and moved east on trails long familiar to the warriors.

They spent the night sleeping without shelter in the woods and rose before daybreak to continue their journey.

The first settlers' cabins were visible from a hillside that they reached at midday. As the men took a brief rest, Walter Butler opened his pack and took out what he said was "clothing suitable to an attorney."

Doffing his uniform, he pulled on tan breeches and gray silk stockings. Sitting on a log, he replaced his military boots with fashionable black leather shoes, fastened with brass buckles. This was followed by a white linen shirt, matching cravat, and a brocaded waistcoat. Finally, he put on a black broadcloth coat and proceeded to smooth out the wrinkles from his tricornered hat, which had required folding to fit into the pack.

Aware of the puzzled looks on his men's faces, Walter said, "Inconvenient though this civilian clothing may be, General St. Leger and I felt that it would make a profound impression on the local inhabitants."

Butler, who had not spoken to Hanyost since he killed the wolf, turned to him.

"Where does your friend Shoemaker live?"

"My friend?"

Now that they were here, it suddenly struck Hanyost that Walter Butler had no plan of his own at all. He had brought a fighting force to this point but now did not have any idea what to do next.

"My cousins said that their father considered him loyal to the King."

"Yes, yes," said Walter impatiently. "Where is his farm?"

"I am not sure. It is near us. On the south bank of the river, about two miles from German Flatts."

"You are not sure?" Walter Butler was growing enraged. "You bring us this far and now you are not sure?"

"Do none of these other men know any loyalists?"

"My men?" Butler was incredulous. "How would they know anyone around here? They are all from Johnstown!"

"I will try to find Shoemaker's farm," said Hanyost. "Let us keep following the river."

At Butler's insistence, the large group stayed together. The Mohawks warned him that they were sure to attract notice in such a relatively populous area, and should split into smaller units, but he would have none of it. "We need to make it clear that we are a disciplined military force and not mere stragglers," he told them. "If we encounter rebel patrols, I will display the flag of truce and explain our purposes. We have nothing to gain by skulking about."

197

Even Hanyost was skeptical about the wisdom of that strategy, but he kept pushing on, taking the lead into increasingly open farm country.

"I think that is Shoemaker's farm," he told Butler an hour later. "I will go first."

"Nonsense," said Butler. "We will arrive in force and displaying the flag of truce."

Pursuant to his orders, the band marched up to the farmhouse. An older man saw them coming and ran inside. A moment later he exited with a woman and two children running as fast as they could. The Mohawks immediately encircled them and the four dropped to their knees in horror. Butler quickly reached them.

"Have no fear," he said, white flag in hand. "Mr. Shoemaker, we have come in peace to seek your help."

Hanyost began to wonder if this was even the Shoemaker farm? He knew it only from his cousins' description.

"I'm not John Shoemaker," the terrified farmer told Butler. "He's about given up farming. He keeps a tavern just over the hill. You'll find him there. Please don't kill us. We're not with the rebels. We're all loyal to the King here."

"Good," said Butler. "I am very glad to hear that. Now, all of you, stand up. Have no fear. You will lead us to Mr. Shoemaker."

"Can my wife and children stay here?" the man pleaded.

"No," said Butler, forcing a smile. "Since you are a loyal family, you should all join us at Mr. Shoemaker's."

Butler and the farmer now took the lead, as the soldiers and Indians marched along the edge of a flourishing cornfield. Hanyost wondered how his own crop fared and pictured his mother anxiously waiting for him at their cabin only a few miles to the east.

And his brother Nicholas? He certainly was not at Oriskany. He must be safe at their uncle's farm, taking care of the livestock and the slaves.

Hanyost was thinking again of the horrors of the battle in the ravine as the group reached a small log cabin built on cleared land between a wooded slope and a cornfield.

"I think you know Hanyost Schuyler," Walter Butler was saying to a stocky, balding man.

John Shoemaker squinted toward him, eyeing his long braided hair. "He looks like an Injun to me."

Hanyost held out his hand. "I am the nephew of Delia Shoemaker, your brother's wife."

"Oh surely," said Shoemaker. "I've heard Delia speak of you. You're the one they all say is crazy."

"That is what they say," returned Hanyost.

The man laughed. "Come inside, all of you who can fit. We'll kill a hog and set up a fine feast for you. We have not had a customer all day, so you're right welcome."

"Can you send word to other loyalists in the vicinity?" asked Butler.

"Other loyalists?" Shoemaker scratched his head. "Oh surely, surely. I'll send my boys out to fetch some of the neighbors who have no use for all this foolishness cooked up by Herkimer and his cronies."

The tavern, though comfortable and well-built, was too small to accommodate the large number of men who had come with Butler. Several of the soldiers carried a long table out into the yard and set up a few chairs around it. The Mohawks, at their most gracious, smiled amiably on Shoemaker's wife and two daughters as they brought out bread and a small keg of beer.

"Have no fear, gallant redskins," said Shoemaker. "When my boys bring back the other guests, I am sure they will come with more victuals and drink."

Additional farmers arrived within the next couple of hours and most did bring food and drink, though nowhere near enough to satisfy the hungry Mohawks. Eventually, a half dozen local men, some with their wives and children, were gathered in the yard.

Walter smoothed his wrinkled suit and stood up to welcome them.

"I am Walter Butler, lieutenant in the Royal Rangers Company commanded by my father, John Butler. These men are soldiers in my company and I am sure you know our loyal allies from Connajoharry. We have come here with a flag of truce under the orders of General Barry St. Leger, commander of the King's forces not thirty miles from here."

"Pleased to meet you," said one grizzled old farmer.

"To continue," said Walter. "General St. Leger has achieved a great victory over the rebel forces led by the traitor Nicholas Herkimer, whom I am sure you all despise as much as I do. Herkimer may saying that he and his treasonous followers won the battle but we are here to inform you that the rebels were totally broken by our brave soldiers and our loyal allies from the Six Nations."

"We knew Herkimer was beat pretty bad," said Shoemaker. "My boy saw them come dragging themselves into Fort Dayton and he said they must have lost hundreds of men up there in Oriskany."

"Such a shame!" his wife began to weep.

"People are saying her brother got killed," explained Shoemaker, patting his wife's knee. "Folks around here are grievin' bad and we're afraid some of Herkimer's boys might do us harm."

"All who are loyal to the King will be safe," said Butler. "Moreover, the King in his mercy will forgive any rebels who lay down their weapons and join us."

"I mean to say," Shoemaker interrupted, "When are you fellows going to bring your army and your Injuns down this way to protect us?"

"General St. Leger will be here within days and will sweep the remnants of Herkimer's force before him. I expect that all the rebels in the valley who do not accept the King's mercy will be hung by this time next week."

"You don't say!"

"General St. Leger now calls upon each and every loyal man to take up his musket and join us in a general rising against the rebels and thieves who now control this region. Together we will cut off the head of the snake of treason!"

"Who are they?" said Hanyost, looking past Butler into the cornfield beyond.

Annoyed at the interruption, Butler frowned at Hanyost.

"And who are they?" Shoemaker pointed toward the wooded hillside in the opposite direction.

Lines of soldiers, clad in light blue and with bayonets fixed, were advancing upon the small tavern from all sides.

Halting twenty yards out, they raised their muskets.

Their leader called out in a loud voice: "Lay down your arms and you will be spared. Resist and you will be shot like dogs."

Evaluating the situation very quickly, the Mohawks placed their muskets and tomahawks on the ground and raised their hands high above them. The rangers looked to Butler for orders. When he gave none, they too lay down their muskets.

"I come with a flag of truce," Walter Butler called out, but by then the Continental troops had reached him and roughly pulled his arms behind him.

"You are all under arrest for treason and spying," said the chief officer.

35. Prisoner of the Continental Army

Shoemaker was knocked to the ground while Butler struggled furiously against two soldiers who quickly bound his arms behind his back. Hanyost found himself shoved from behind and lost his footing. He was quickly forced to the ground, his face in the dirt and his arms tightly lashed together.

The soldiers had soon subdued all of Shoemaker's guests. One of them gave Hanyost a kick in the ribs before moving on to provide the same treatment to the man next to him. "Murderin' savages, the whole lot of you!" he said. "We ought to hang you right here from one of your own apple trees."

"What's this one, a white man or a savage?" The lanky soldier whom the others called Murphy picked up Hanyost's bow and hurled it far out into the cornfield. Grabbing a fistful of the painstakingly crafted arrows, he broke them over his knee.

Stooping, he picked up the tomahawk Brant had given to Hanyost and examined the blade. "Looks like fresh blood to me."

"What do you think, boys?" He held it out for examination.

"Sure, it's blood," said one.

"Let's hang this one here and now."

"Wish we could do it, boys," their officer said. "They all deserve hanging, I'll agree. But Colonel Weston wants us to bring 'em in for questioning."

Hanyost and the others were pulled roughly to their feet, shoved and cursed a few more times, and set on their way, marching rapidly eastward, each prisoner accompanied by a man with a musket at his back.

"Easy now," Tenbrook kept telling a soldier who was prodding him in the back with a bayonet.

Hanyost noticed that one of the farmers from the tavern was unbound and walked along freely, chatting with the soldiers.

The sun was still high as the palisades of Fort Dayton came in view. A mix of militia and regular army soldiers manned the new stronghold, hastily erected near German Flatts. Hanyost saw men crowding the firing platforms of the palisades, the militia in buckskins or homespun and the soldiers in new blue jackets.

A short, barrel-chested man in a blue jacket greeted Hanyost's captors at the foot of the palisade. "We got 'em, Colonel Weston, sir," reported the man who acted as leader of their captors. " Didn't have to kill a one of 'em, neither."

"Good work, men," said Weston. "Line them up and let's see what kind of fish we pulled in." Weston strode down the ragged line of captives, whose arms remained tied behind their backs.

"Shoemaker," Weston greeted the farmer. "You're quite a generous fellow when it comes to entertaining traitors, aren't you?"

The colonel turned to a young soldier who followed at his heels, balancing a quill, a bottle of ink and a ledger book. "Note it down. Shoemaker. Chief traitor and organizer of the conspiracy."

Weston walked a few more steps before coming to a sudden halt. "What do we have here? Walter Butler, himself!"

"I must request that you unbind my arms," Butler said as coolly as he could under the circumstances. "I have come here under a flag of truce with the most peaceful of intentions."

"I think Mr. Petrie will tell us a different story," said Weston, indicating the farmer who had accompanied us from Shoemaker's. "As soon as he received your invitation to treason, he sent his boy running to let us know. And now Mr. Petrie is telling us everything you said in your little speech."

"I have been sent by General Barry St. Leger to enter into negotiations," Walter Butler maintained.

"And he sent you in that fine suit? If you are a soldier, you are out of uniform, and by the rules of war you are a spy. And spies hang. Your own generals would agree. That's why they hung that poor lad from Connecticut, Nathan Hale, last year."

"I am wearing this clothing because I am a lawyer as well as an officer of the King," he tried to explain. "In negotiating with the good subjects in this region, I am acting as a lawyer, that is to say, as an advocate for the King."

"Is that why you asked Shoemaker and his lot to take up muskets against us?"

Weston raised his voice to address everyone, those leaning over the palisade wall and those gathered on the field before the fort. "This here is Walter Butler. Him and his old man are among the worst of the Tories. He has led his fellow traitors and bloodthirsty Injuns in the killing and butchering of his own neighbors. Humanity will shed no tears over the hanging of this man, which is going to happen very shortly."

"I came here in good faith under a flag of truce," Butler continued to protest. "By the rules of law, which you appear to know so well, you cannot hold me as a prisoner."

"Rules of war!" Weston exploded. "Is that what you call killing the wounded and defenseless?"

"We cannot always control our native allies."

Shaking his head, the colonel proceeded down the line, asking the name of each captured soldier as his assistant noted it in the ledger book. When he reached Tenbrook, the man pointed out that he was captured while in uniform. "I am not a spy and I was not at Oriskany."

Ignoring him, Weston looked over the Mohawks. "Write down twelve savages," he said. "Common Indians, I'd say by the way they keep their mouths shut. If any of 'em was chiefs they'd be making long speeches by now."

He came to the last man, who happened to be Hanyost. "Now what species of traitor are you? You're dressed like a savage and you have no uniform. I'd guess you're a spy, plain and simple."

"I am Hanyost Schuyler, sir," he mumbled, his accent growing thicker the more afraid he became. "It was my idea to come here and tell the people not to fight any more. I want peace for people."

"Oho, a peacemaker?" Weston turned to his men for an appreciative laugh. "You'll be singing us a psalm next, I'll wager."

"I did not kill anyone at Oriskany ravine."

"Oh no?" Weston brought his face close to Hanyost's. "If so, then why are you denying what I have not yet accused you of?"

Hanyost did not know how to answer him.

Tim Murphy stepped forward and handed Colonel Weston the tomahawk he had taken from Hanyost. "I took this off him, sir. You'll see that the blood is pretty fresh."

Weston examined the blade. "Did you use this on your own good Christian neighbors? Were you at Oriskany?"

"Yes, but I did not..."

"Were you on Butler's side or ours?"

"I was not..."

"I know that man!" one of the militiamen called down from the parapet. "He's Herkimer's nephew, the one who deserted to the Tories. I seen him at Oriskany. Ran right past us, he did, and I woulda shot him but that my powder had got wet."

Hanyost tried to see who had identified him.

"I ran to shoot an arrow at Joseph Brant..." Hanyost tried to explain, calling up toward the parapet.

"You're claiming that you killed Brant?" scoffed Weston.

"No, I did not but..."

Weston instructed his aide. "Write down this man's name and note particularly that he came disguised as an Indian and admits to being a deserter and to taking up arms against the United States. I'd say him and Butler are the most qualified to hang of any of them."

"You can't possibly mean to hang us," Butler shouted. "You have no authority to impose a capital sentence. I am an officer of the King and I am here under a flag of truce."

Weston strolled back to stand face to face with Walter Butler. "I don't plan to hang you myself, Mr. Butler. I will wait until General Benedict Arnold arrives in a day or two with a thousand more Continentals. I'll let him decide how high to hang you and how short the rope!"

36. In Chains
August 15 – 16, 1777

"Hate to put chains on a white man," said Tim Murphy as he latched heavy iron cuffs onto Hanyost's wrists. "Don't seem right, somehow."

Hanyost was struck by an unexpected note of sympathy in Murphy's voice.

"You're pretty young, aintcha?" asked Murphy as he ran a chain through a pair of leg cuffs. "How'd you get mixed up with the likes of that bigmouth?"

"I wanted to stop the war," Hanyost explained. "I went to Fort Stanwix because I thought that people there were talking about peace."

"Maybe you just ain't too bright," continued Murphy as he finished tightening the leg irons on Walter Butler, who glared silently at him.

The soldier paused by the door of the shed in which the two were imprisoned. "Too bad you'll prob'ly hang, young fella."

"My friend told me this would happen." Hanyost thought of Ataentsic and how he would never see her again.

"You got a smart friend," said Murphy. "You got any family?"

"My mother and my brother." Hanyost pictured his mother. "Can you send word to her that I am here?"

"She   live   'round   here?"

"Yes, our cabin is near Connajoharry, six or seven miles downriver."

"I'll see what I can do," said Murphy. "There's usually some hangers-on around the fort. I'll ask if anyone could go tell your ma."

"I thank you," said Hanyost. He wanted to see his mother one last time before he died.

Murphy bolted shut the heavy wooden door of the shed. A few minutes later, his voice could be heard in the yard outside. "I need somebody to take a message to the mother of one of these traitors. I'll give ya a shilling." When there was no response, he bellowed. "All right! Two shillings, and it's outta my own pocket!"

"Why didn't they keep us with the other prisoners?" Hanyost asked Walter Butler later that day.

Butler looked at him with contempt, shaking his head. "Because it's us they plan to hang, you fool! They'll probably try to exchange the others for the captives we have up at Fort Stanwix."

"Will they truly hang us?" Hanyost imagined the rope tightening around his neck.

"I expect they will."

They were silent for a while before Butler added, "I was a fool to listen to a simpleton like you! You really are feeble-minded, do you know that?"

"This is what white people have always said," Hanyost answered calmly. He was beginning to imagine the Plentiful Country that Black Jacob had described to him, a deep forest abounding in deer, streams full of salmon as in the old days before the whites had come. All the tribes dwelling in peace in one great longhouse. His father would be there with his many Iroquois friends. Dying will not be so bad. It will be a good thing.

The next morning Murphy brought them tin plates of beef stew. He pulled up a stool and sat with them as they ate. "Pretty good grub, ain't it?"

"It is," agreed Hanyost. "Better than they have at Fort Stanwix."

"You prob'ly didn't hear the news?"

"News?"

"Yes, word came in that Nick Herkimer died. Seems he got gangrene in his leg. A fancy new surgeon cut off the leg and bungled the job. He bled to death."

"I am sad to hear this," Hanyost said. "He was my uncle."

"No foolin'?" marveled Murphy. "The big general hereabouts was your uncle and you still end up on the wrong side?"

"Yes." Hanyost put his spoon down. "Is my mother coming?"

"I found a half-Injun fella agreed to go tell her you was here. I expect he'll do it if he wants the coin I promised him."

The morning passed very slowly as Hanyost sat leaning against the roughly hewn wall. Through a crack in the logs, he could see uniformed soldiers and militia going and coming in the yard. Everyone seemed to know his task. Even the few Indian allies, who appeared to be Oneidas, were purposeful. He thought about the difficulties St. Leger had in controlling a far larger number of Indians.

"There are Oneida warriors here," he observed to Butler.

Walter Butler ignored him.

"These men do not let their Oneida friends kill or torture prisoners," Hanyost persisted. "They did not give us to the Oneidas."

"Sounds like you want to change sides again, is that it?" Butler glared at him. "Why don't you go ahead and try? See if it saves you from having your neck twisted."

Hanyost continued to observe the yard. The more he thought about what he saw, the more he contrasted it with St. Leger's camp. Slowly, an idea began to take shape for him.

Then he saw his mother coming across the yard. She seemed to have aged greatly in the few weeks he had been gone. She leaned heavily on his brother Nicholas. Tim Murphy met them and spoke intently to her, gesturing toward the makeshift jail from where Hanyost watched. Another soldier joined them and led Elizabeth and Nicholas toward the central blockhouse. A ragged man approached Murphy and he gave him some coins.

A moment later Murphy was unbarring the door. "Your ma is here, young fella, and your brother. Colonel Weston needs to speak with 'em but they'll be here presently."

For over an hour Hanyost peered through the crack in the logs. Men came and went from the commander's cabin but still his mother and brother did not emerge. Finally, he saw his mother and even at that distance, she seemed badly shaken. A few minutes later, Murphy brought her and his brother to their cell.

"Sorry fer the intrusion, but Colonel Weston was most particular that I remain here with you folks while you talk," said Murphy, stepping aside to allow Elizabeth to enter the small room. "Sit down, ma'am," said Murphy, placing a stool on the floor. "Please."

When Nicholas tried to follow her, Murphy blocked him with his elbow. "Sorry, young fella, you stay outside fer now."

Elizabeth threw her arms around Hanyost and wept loudly. "Your uncle Nicholas is dead,' she told him.

"I know, Ma, I know."

"And you're to be hanged!" She burst into tears.

"I know, Ma."

Finally, Elizabeth grew calmer, still breathing deeply.

"Nicholas and I pleaded with the Colonel, but he said he could do nothing. He's waiting for General Arnold to come."

"I think you'll have a long wait for that particular officer!" laughed Butler, who had been leaning sullenly against the wall. "Even Schuyler would not be so great a fool as to divide his army in the face of General Burgoyne's mighty force."

Murphy grabbed him by the neck and hurled him, chains clanking into the yard. "Watch this one close, will ya?" he called to someone out of view.

"He needn't be present for this reunion of mother and son," said Murphy. "Pay him no mind."

"Mother, I saw Uncle Johan," said Hanyost.

"He lives?"

"Yes, but he's a captive inside Fort Stanwix."

His mother continued to weep.

A thought occurred to Hanyost. "Does the Colonel want me to tell him anything?" he asked Murphy.

"No, I don't think he needs you to say anything. Them that came with you had plenty to say, especially that Tenbrook fella. Not much you could add to all he's been sayin'."

"What did Tenbrook say?"

"Oh, he went on about how the Injuns are gettin' fed up and how there's not much food and scarcely a tent left since Willett made his raid."

"That is true."

"Marinus Willett snuck out of the fort right under your noses, did you know that?"

"He did?"

"Sure, he was here a couple days ago and then he kept going to report to General Arnold down in Albany."

"General Arnold is coming?"

"That's what the Colonel says. Only I'm wonderin' if yer friend Butler is right. General Schuyler might not let him go, what with Burgoyne bearing down on Albany. Schuyler sure don't want to be left shorthanded to face the redcoats."

"The English general St. Leger should go home."

Murphy looked quizzically at Hanyost. "Don't think that's too likely, boy."

"General St. Leger and all who are with him should go home."

"Here, why'n't ya talk with your brother?" Murphy motioned for Nicholas to enter the small shed.

"I have explained to Colonel Weston that you were never a Tory," said his brother, putting his arms around him. "I tried to explain to him that Uncle Nicholas was mistaken in reporting that you were a deserter."

"Thank you, Nicholas," said Hanyost trying to raise his manacled hand to grasp his brother's. "But I think they are determined to hang me unless…"

"Unless?"

"Unless I can think of a way to end the fighting…"

Depiction of Elizabeth Schuyler pleading with Benedict Arnold for
the life of her son, from *The Mohawk Valley During the Revolution*
by Harold Frederic, 1877

37. A Mother's Plea
August 21, 1777

Three days later, another, noticeably less friendly, soldier, brought a meager breakfast to Hanyost and Butler. "Won't be long now,' the soldier commented as he dropped two tins of porridge on the floor of their jail.

"Won't be long?" asked Hanyost.

"Til General Arnold is here. Chances are he'll hold court and have you two at the end of a rope before nightfall."

"Can I see my mother?" asked Hanyost. He had watched her waiting forlornly near the blockhouse since first light.

"I'm sure you can see her one more time before ya swing."

"Tim Murphy lets her come to see me each day."

"Murphy ain't here. He's gone out with a troop to greet General Arnold and provide an escort to him and his boys," said the soldier, slamming and bolting the door behind him.

The morning dragged on and grew warm and humid as Hanyost stood by the crack in the logs, watching as his mother tried to talk with various officers who came and left the blockhouse. Around midmorning he saw that Nicholas had joined her.

At noon the fort's cannons sounded. Butler leapt up, thinking that a rescue force had arrived, but the cheering of the soldiers told them that the firing had only been a salute to greet the arrival of Benedict Arnold and his officers. Soldiers and civilians swarmed to the firing platforms to watch the approaching troops. The sounds of fife and drum could be heard in the distance.

Hanyost could barely see the edge of the main gate as it swung open to admit several horsemen. General Arnold was immediately identifiable as he leapt down from his stallion and tossed the reins to Nicholas, whom he evidently took for a groom.

"Plenty of fresh oats for my charger, lad," his voice boomed across the milling yard. "He's had a hard ride."

Officers and men thronged about the general, pumping his hand. Arnold patiently greeted them all.

"Weston, good fellow!" cried Benedict Arnold, recognizing the colonel as he pushed his way through the crowd. "Let's to work. There's much to do if we're to vanquish the foe!"

The crowd surged behind Arnold and Weston as they entered the blockhouse, pressing up against the narrow gun ports trying to catch a glimpse of the two leaders.

Nicholas stood uncertainly, grasping the reins of Arnold's restless horse. More Continentals jammed into the courtyard and were surrounded by the fort's garrison. In the tumult, Hanyost lost sight of his mother and Nicholas.

Several Indians, clearly part of Arnold's force, remained at the edge of the crowd.

"He has Indians with him," Hanyost said to Butler. "Probably Oneida or Tuscarora scouts."

Hanyost's attention was caught by one of the scouts, a tall muscular Indian in buckskins and a cast-off Continental jacket. His face was away from Hanyost. Who was he? Then he turned to exchange a joke with two of his fellows.

Onatah!

Nicholas emerged from the throng, pulled forward by Arnold's horse. People jumped out of the way to avoid being crushed. Onatah reached for the reins and helped Nicholas restrain the stallion.

They recognized each other. Hanyost's mother joined them. As the three spoke, Elizabeth motioned toward the shed where Hanyost was imprisoned. Onatah nodded and spoke very seriously to Elizabeth.

"My old friend is there," said Hanyost. "He will try to help us."

Butler glared at him, saying nothing.

The crowd continued to mill about, until the officers finally managed to get the Continentals to rejoin their units. Hanyost saw Tim Murphy arguing with an officer before finally being persuaded to leave. Someone came and led away Arnold's horse. Onatah and three of his Indian companions remained with Hanyost's mother and brother in the dwindling crowd of civilians and militia outside the blockhouse.

After about two hours, four soldiers unlocked the door of the shed and roughly pulled Hanyost and Butler out into the yard, quickly marching them toward the blockhouse. Hanyost saw his mother and Nicholas. Onatah called out in Mohawk. "I am here, my brother-by-another-mother."

As they reached the blockhouse, the door opened and out stepped Arnold. He was a short compact man with dark blazing eyes. "We'll hold the court martial in public, so all may see and learn from the fate of traitors and spies," he announced. "Set up a table and some chairs, there in the center of the yard, and get to work erecting the gallows!"

In minutes Arnold was seated behind a table, Weston to his left and another, lantern-jawed officer to his right. Hanyost and Butler stood in their chains, two soldiers firmly grasping each of them. Continentals with muskets pushed back the crowd of civilians into a large circle around the table.

"Colonel Weston, commander of this post and Colonel Willett, on special assignment from the brave defenders of Fort Stanwix, and I will constitute a summary tribunal, herewith convened by authority of the Continental Congress to judge charges brought against the spies and traitors Walter N. Butler and..." Arnold searched for a name until Weston whispered in his ear. "...and the deserter from the Tryon County Militia, Hanyost Schuyler. Colonel Willett, as presiding officer, will now read the charges."

"Five days since, a loyal patriot, Mr. George Petrie sent word to this fort that a traitorous meeting had been hatched at the farm of John Shoemaker. Colonel Weston promptly dispatched a force of men which apprehended Walter Butler and Hanyost Schuyler in civilian garb, accompanied by twelve members of John Johnson's company in addition to a dozen savages. I call Mr. Petrie to act as witness to the nature of the aforesaid traitorous meeting."

The farmer came forward, placed his hand on a Bible held by Willett and launched into a thorough description of Butler's arrival and speech at Shoemaker's tavern.

"To conclude," said Petrie after ten minutes, "This here Butler asked us to get our muskets and set upon and kill our patriot neighbors, promising us all great riches if we would do this devilish work."

"Thank you, Mr. Petrie, for doing your patriotic duty," said Arnold. "Colonel Weston, are there other witnesses?"

"Yes, sir, there are. I call Private John Shults of the Tryon County militia, a true patriot who fought at Oriskany and saw many of his brave neighbors butchered by the Tories and savages."

Private Shults stepped forward, placed his hand on the Bible and swore to tell the whole truth and nothing but the truth, so help him God.

"Private Shults," said Arnold. "What can you tell us about these two?"

"General, sir, I was at Oriskany and I seen it all. I seen Walter Butler leading his butchering Tories and I seen this man Hanyost Schuyler."

"Butler was acting as an officer of the aforesaid Tories?"

"Yes, sir. When the shootin' begun, I seen Butler come running through the trees. I seen him shoot a man dead. And they killed men who was wounded. When it rained and our muskets were too wet to shoot, Butler and his devils found our wounded men and killed them on the spot with their tomahawks."

"How about this other man?" asked Willett.

"I seen him too, clear as day. It was during the rainstorm when I saw him running through the trees with his bow and arrows, that savage!"

"And to your knowledge, is he a deserter from the Tryon County Militia."

"Yes sir, a fellow with me recognized him and said he deserted from Captain Demuth's company. His own uncle, General Herkimer, God rest his soul, reported him to General Schuyler. Deserted with the late general's treacherous brother, Johan Herkimer, he did."

"And that fellow you speak of who knew this, is he here?"

"No sir, he got killed near the end of the day when the Tories turned their coats and tried to fool us, but we spotted their dirty trick and blasted away at them."

"Thank you, Private Shults," said Arnold. "Now, are there any witnesses for the defense?"

When no one spoke up, he explained. "Is there anyone here to put in a word as to why we shouldn't hang these two?"

"I will."

Hanyost heard his mother's voice before he saw her. She came forward slowly, with Nicholas supporting her by the arm.

"And what is your connection to this matter?" asked Arnold.

"I am Hanyost's Schuyler's mother."

"And I am his brother," Nicholas added.

"And what can you add to our knowledge of the circumstances of this case?"

"I ask you to have mercy on him." His mother burst into tears and could go no further.

"He never deserted," said Nicholas. "My uncle was mistaken when he reported that my brother was a deserter. Hanyost was a ranger for Captain Demuth, that's true, and he was sent on patrols. Captain Demuth can tell you."

"And is Captain Demuth here?" asked Arnold.

"Hannes Demuth was one of the brave messengers General Herkimer sent to Fort Stanwix," said Willett, "and remains there yet contributing to the defense."

"Well, then," said Arnold, "while I fully understand your desire to speak on behalf of your son and brother, nothing that you have said constitutes evidence. Is there anyone else who has something to say on behalf of these two?"

"I speak now."

Hanyost recognized Onatah's heavily accented English.

"Injuns are not permitted to testify in court," said Weston. "Stand back, you savage."

"This particular Indian can testify here," snapped Arnold. "He is one of my loyal Tuscaroras and I'd trust him with my life. Onatah, come up here and put your hand on this Bible."

Onatah placed his hand on the book Arnold held out to him.

"Do you swear by the Lord Jehovah and any other heathen deities you may worship to tell the whole truth or else go straight to hellfire?"

"Yes."

"Good enough for me," said Arnold. "Now tell us what you know."

"I know nothing of this one." He pointed to Butler. "But this one is my brother."

"Your brother?" laughed Willett. "You two don't look much alike, do you?"

"He is my brother in the way of our people," Onatah explained. "He is friend of my people. He learn our ways. When I have trouble and almost die, he save my life. I give my life for his."

Arnold smiled. "Onatah, you are a man who knows what it is to be loyal and I place great value on that virtue. I admire your loyalty to your blood brother Schuyler, but this is not evidence, do you understand?"

Onatah shook his head.

"Your old friend has committed a crime against the United States. Nothing you have said changes that. I know that you would give your life to save a friend but you cannot help him. Now step back."

"Since there are no witnesses for the defense, I will give the defendants a chance to speak for themselves. Mr. Butler, you go first."

"Lieutenant Walter Butler, sir, if you please."

"Lieutenant Butler, then. Please, speak."

"As I told this officer," he jerked his jaw toward Weston, chains clanking. "I came here under a flag of truce to conduct peace negotiations with the good people of this valley. I was detained and imprisoned illegally and, under the rules of war, I demand that I be immediately released from your custody and permitted to return to my regiment."

"I see," Arnold said, reviewing a paper that Weston placed in front of him. "The evidence already presented contradicts your assertion, Lieutenant Butler. May I ask if Mr. Schuyler has anything to say?"

"I came for peace but I was wrong," said Hanyost.

" I see, " said Arnold. "Same story as the other one."

Arnold turned to his two fellow officers. "Are we in agreement as to the verdict?" Weston and Willett nodded. "Both are guilty as charged."

"Therefore, by the power invested in this tribunal by the Continental Congress of the United Sates of America, we find the defendants Walter Butler and Hanyost Schuyler guilty and sentence them to be hung by the neck until dead, sentence to be carried out as soon as we can finish setting up the gallows."

Engraving of Benedict Arnold by Thomas Hart, 1776

38. The Gallows
August 21, 1777

"Leave the prisoners out here in the yard," said Colonel Weston. "They can watch the gallows being built. But keep a close watch on them."

Turning to Arnold, he said, moving toward the blockhouse, "Now, back to our council. We have much to decide before we are ready to march."

"Let's hold our council of war out here in the yard," said Arnold. "At least there's a bit of a breeze. It's sweltering in your quarters, Colonel."

"Very well, General. I'll just have my men shoo all these hangers-on past the palisade so we can speak in confidence."

As the Continentals herded the civilians, including Hanyost's mother and brother, away, the prisoners' guards looped their chains around a hitching post. Two other men appeared, carrying a pair of large beams from the other side of the stockade. "I never built no gallows," said one.

"Neither did I," said the other. "What say we just set up a couple beams as supports and one across the top. Shouldn't take long."

"We have to dig a couple of pits to hold the beams in place."

"Right," laughed the other. "Wouldn't do to have this pair o'rogues come crashin' down with the ropes round their necks, not hardly dead at all."

Hanyost looked over at Butler, who was listening to this conversation with horror. He decided against offering a word of comfort about the Plentiful Country to which they would both soon be going.

Once the courtyard was cleared, Arnold, Weston and Willett were joined by several other officers, including Colonel Peter Bellinger of the Tryon County Militia. Hanyost nodded to him, but was ignored. Huge horseflies were buzzing around Hanyost's face but he had no way to brush them away.

"So, Colonel Willett, why don't we start by reviewing the situation at Fort Stanwix," began Arnold.

"When I left the fort two days after the battle," said Willett, "St. Leger had resumed firing with his light cannon and mortars. But I do not believe that he will be able to breach the walls with such ordnance."

"And what is the state of the garrison?"

"Colonel Gansevoort remains staunch in his determination to resist the enemy, as are all of the defenders. Food, powder and musket ball are in adequate supply, although ball for the cannons is not."

"What of St. Leger's force? Is it true that he sustained only light casualties against the militia?"

"I am afraid that is the truth," said Bellinger. "Although we held the field at close of battle on August 6th, the enemy lost nowhere near as many men as we did. They attacked from the cover of the forest and we sustained our heaviest losses in the very first minutes of the onslaught. After that we fought back well enough, but I'd say they lost less than a hundred killed or wounded."

"You are saying that St. Leger still has a formidable force. How many would you estimate?"

"Perhaps two thousand," said Willett. "A mix of redcoats, Hessians, and Tories numbering a thousand and an additional thousand savages."

"That would mean that St. Leger still outnumbers my nine hundred men by at least two to one." Arnold stared into the distance. "General Schuyler badly needs every one of them to meet Burgoyne and that meeting is no more than weeks away."

"How many men can you raise from the militia, Colonel Bellinger?" asked Willett.

"Sir, to my great embarrassment, I must say that we would be fortunate to raise even half of the one hundred and fifty who returned with me from Oriskany. Many have already gone back to their farms. Of course, Jacob Klock is now in command and he could tell you more."

"And where is Colonel Klock?"

"At present I believe he has gone to Connajoharry, the Mohawk village, to search for suspected spies."

"Weston, how many can you spare from the garrison here?" Arnold asked.

"I cannot leave the fort too lightly garrisoned, sir," explained Weston. "We have the lives of several hundred civilians to protect. At most, I could detach fifty men."

The meeting lapsed into silence as Arnold pondered what the officers had told him. Hanyost watched him closely, no longer hearing the hammering behind him as several soldiers worked to build the gallows. A thought grew in him.

"Of course, I can beat St. Leger's motley band of savages and traitors," said Arnold. "We would have to approach the fort more cautiously than brave Herkimer did, sending out my loyal Tuscarora and Oneida scouts well in advance. Even if the enemy did lay for us in the ravine, we could fight our way through."

"Yes, sir," said Bellinger.

Just then a messenger was admitted to the fort. The man, breathing heavily, handed a folded paper to Arnold. He broke the seal and read it quickly, frowning.

"Well, well, Lieutenant Butler," he said, reddening with anger. "It seems you have friends in high places."

Butler simply looked at him. The men building the gallows paused to listen.

"This note is from General Schuyler. It appears that your well-placed friends in Albany have interceded on your behalf. You are not to be hung, not just yet, anyway. Men, take him back to the jail and lock him up. Once we have done with the present business, we're to send this traitor and spy to Albany where his case will be reviewed."

"What of the other traitor?" asked Weston.

"Oh, we can hang him," said Arnold. "He'll provide a good enough example of the penalty for treason."

Hanyost watched the soldiers lead Butler back to the shed that served as the fort's jail. The men behind him resumed building the gallows, pulling the cross beam up with great effort. He saw Onatah with three Indian companions, waiting for Arnold at the far end of the stockade. When his friend tried to come closer, a soldier barred him with a raised musket.

Benedict Arnold resumed the conference with the other officers. "And is the military road through Oriskany ravine the only way to approach Fort Stanwix?"

"It is the only way other than cutting a new road through the woods. That is, if you wanted to bring your horses and cannon. Men could walk through the woods and marshes, I suppose, if you left the baggage train behind."

"No, Bellinger, we'll need our horse and light cannon if we are to meet St. Leger on the open field before the fort. That's a lesson I learned at Montreal in '75. I'm leery, too, of having my men scattered all about the woods where the savages can pick them off one by one. I've trained them to fight in units and they're not practiced in the Indian style of war."

"So we will proceed along the military road, as General Herkimer did, but with more caution, is that your intent?" asked Bellinger.

"I see no alternative," replied Arnold, "though I am loath to lose the time and men that may be the difference between victory and defeat against Burgoyne's army."

"We hear that Burgoyne has a much larger army than St. Leger's," said Weston.

"True, but if we can crush Burgoyne, this war may well be over. If Burgoyne triumphs, the colonies will be cut in half and the war will end in our defeat. Then we'll be the ones facing the gallows, like this young lad." He glanced over at Hanyost.

"Sir?" said Hanyost. "I have spent many days in the camp of St. Leger. I know how the soldiers and the Indian people are feeling."

"I thought we had heard the last from this prisoner," snapped Weston. "Soldier, go find a rag to stop his mouth."

"No," said Arnold, raising his hand. "I would hear him."

"Sir," Hanyost burst out in a torrent of words. "The Indian people who are with General St. Leger are very angry and he cannot make them do as he says. There are more Indian people than you think, and not so many whites."

"Pray, continue," urged Arnold.

"If you let me go to them, I will tell them that you have a great army with many soldiers and that all of the Indian people will be killed. They will leave the English general. He will not be able to make them stay. And without them, he will go back to Canada."

"Rubbish!" spat Weston. "This traitor only wants to save his own neck."

"Tell me," said Arnold, "more about why St. Leger's Indian allies are angry."

"They are angry because Colonel Willett destroyed their camp and took away many things they wanted to keep. They have no tents in which to sleep, no kettles in which to cook their food."

"That may be true,' said Willett. "We did serious damage to their camp in the sortie I led."

"They are also angry because General St. Leger did not want them to hurt and kill the prisoners."

"What have those fiends done to our men?" Bellinger was enraged.

"The Indian people took many captives and killed many. Others they burned with slow fires. I heard they ate the flesh of the captives but I did not see this. St. Leger told them they could only do this to twelve prisoners but they wanted more. So they kept more than twelve. St. Leger could not stop them. The Senecas and Cayugas are very angry at the white people because of the warriors who were killed in Oriskany ravine."

"All this may be true," said Willett, "but there is no likelihood that the Indians will believe anything this fellow says."

"They will believe Hanyost Schuyler!" Onatah stepped forward. "He speaks the Mohawk language. He spent many days as a child in our village. All of the Mohawk people know him. Thayendenegea knows him."

"Joseph Brant will believe me," said Hanyost. "I....I saved his life in the fighting at Oriskany. He believes that I am meant to protect his life."

"I will go with him. I will say the same thing," said Onatah.

"We cannot trust this Indian any more than we can trust this turncoat," said Bellinger. "Schuyler betrayed his own uncle and he will betray us, if we let him."

Arnold leaned forward, his chin on his hand. "Weston, send someone to look for this man's mother and brother. I am sure they'll be lingering near the gate."

"Onatah," he called his scout forward. "You know that there is great trust in my heart for you."

"Yes, general," he replied.

"You believe that this stratagem – this trick – might work?"

"Yes, general."

"And I know that Hanyost is an old friend of yours?"

Onatah nodded.

"But many years have passed since the days when you were boys together, true?"

"Yes." Onatah was not comfortable with long conversations with English and he strained to follow the general's reasoning.

Arnold looked closely at Onatah. "Yet you still would trust him with your life?"

"Yes."

"You are a good judge of character, my red friend," said Arnold, "and I am inclined to allow you and Hanyost to try this stratagem."

"General, I have to say…" Willett began.

"And I, as well…" said Weston.

"Oh, I know it's not likely to have any effect, gentlemen," Arnold interrupted the two colonels, "but it certainly cannot hurt to throw a bit of fear into the bloodthirsty savages, while I'm readying my forces for the march to Fort Stanwix."

"Ah, Mrs. Schuyler!" Arnold rose to extend his hand to Hanyost's mother, who was escorted forward by two soldiers. "Very good of you to join us. You, too, young Nicholas."

Elizabeth looked uncertainly from the general to her son, her eyes red from weeping. "Can you spare the life of my son?"

"Yes, ma'am, I believe I can." He patted her hand. "Provided that he performs a service for us which will redeem all his past offenses."

"Take the chains off the prisoner!" General Arnold shouted to the soldiers who were hammering together the gallows. "And leave off work on that infernal device. We may not need it just yet."

As the chains were removed from his wrists and ankles, Hanyost stood up, stumbling a little.

"These two lads," said Arnold, stepping around the table in order to throw his arms about the shoulders of Hanyost and his Iroquois friend, "have agreed to perform a most important service for the United States."

Walking back and forth, his arms draped over their shoulders, Arnold seemed more like a fond father than a man who had just condemned Elizabeth's son to death. "Yes, I will indeed spare your son Hanyost from hanging if he goes on this mission and forgive all his many treasonous offenses to boot!"

"There is only one condition I make and it does closely affect your family, ma'am." He stopped pacing and grew deadly serious.

"One condition?" Elizabeth asked.

"I will spare Hanyost from hanging if...."

"If?"

"If his brother Nicholas remains here and agrees to being hung in Hanyost's stead should he fail to complete his mission."

39. A Brother's Life

Nicholas Schuyler could not believe what he was hearing. "Hang me? But I am not a traitor. I….General Herkimer is…was my uncle…"

"Merely a precaution, Mr. Schuyler," said Arnold. "I am sure that you trust your brother to do his duty in this matter."

"General…" Elizabeth began, looking from one son to the other. "Surely, you cannot be…."

"Come, let me talk with this family in private," said Arnold. "Come in to Colonel Weston's quarters. You, as well, Onatah."

Once inside the cramped surroundings of the blockhouse, the general made sure that a seat was found for Elizabeth. Then, leaning on a barrel of gunpowder, he placed a hand on Nicholas' shoulder. "As I said, Mr. Schuyler, this is only a precaution, but you understand that my fellow officers do not have my faith in Hanyost and in his Indian brother Onatah."

"We will do this," said Hanyost. "We will not fail."

"Splendid, just what I need to hear," said Arnold. "I am sure that your brother has nothing to fear."

"But then why…?" asked Elizabeth.

"As I was saying, my fellow officers would look very dubiously on my setting free a convicted spy without any guarantee. And I assure you that I must have the absolute confidence of every one of my officers and men as I lead them into the battlefield which so recently claimed the lives of the flower of the local militia, including your own dear brother, ma'am."

"If I fail, you can hang me," said Hanyost. "But I will not."

"We make a good plan," said Onatah. "We shoot musket balls through your shirt and you say you escape from fort.

"A capital suggestion. We will arrange a false escape, fire some shots so that any spies lurking about will be convinced of the truth of this tale."

"Then," said Onatah, "Hanyost will go first into the enemy camp and tell the story. Then I will come to the camp with the same story. They will all be afraid and will go back to Canada, as my brother says."

"So, Mr. Schuyler, are you convinced?" asked Arnold.

"I don't know." Nicholas felt faint and had to sit down.

"Nicholas," said Hanyost. "I will not let them hang you."

Nicholas looked up at his brother, his expression impossible to read.

"Nicholas, I would not ask you to do this only to save my life," Hanyost tried to explain. "If I can do this, it will save many lives. I saw many men die at Oriskany ravine. More will die if the two sides fight again in that place of death."

"Of course, we would defeat them. That has never been in question," said Arnold. "But you understand that we must try to preserve all of our strength to overcome the greater army that Burgoyne commands."

"General," Elizabeth pleaded. "Let me be hung in Hanyost's place if he fails."

"My dear Mrs. Schuyler, you are a most generous soul and a truly loving mother. But I could not even threaten to hang a lady. No one would believe such a notion were any more than a ruse on my part. No, it is either Nicholas or no one."

Elizabeth looked at her older son, a silent plea in her eyes.

"All right," Nicholas sighed. "I will stay here in your stead, Hanyost. I'm counting on you not to let me hang."

"Thank you," said Hanyost. "I will not let you die."

After the small family had a few more moments together, Arnold had a soldier take Nicholas away. "Lock him up, but not with Butler or any of the others. And find Mrs. Schuyler comfortable quarters."

When they were gone, Arnold called in the other officers and explained the scheme to them. "It may not have any effect at all," he said to Weston and Willett, "but it certainly can do no harm to sow a bit of confusion in the ranks of the enemy."

"If you think so…" Weston remained skeptical.

"I need to wait here at least a day or two until the baggage train catches up with us, so if these two leave today, they can be at Fort Stanwix by tomorrow. In the meantime, I will send my other loyal redskins to reconnoiter the terrain and disposition of the enemy's forces."

"Onatah," he turned to his scout. "It would be wise for you to approach the fort from a different direction. I suggest that you leave now. As for you, Hanyost, I think we'll stage our little drama in an hour, as soon as I can find Tim Murphy.

"I know Tim Murphy."

"He is the best marksman I have and will be an essential player in our little act. In the meantime, you can rest here. I anticipate that you will travel all night."

As Arnold returned to his conference with the other officers, they unrolled a large map and leaned over it.

"This is the route I took in escaping the fort," Willett pointed to the map. "But we can move directly forward along the river, provided that we make full use of extensive flanking parties on our right. We should take some, but not all, of the cannon in the event that we do meet St. Leger before the fort, but remember that Gansevoort can provide covering fire from the ramparts…"

Despite his anxiety and eagerness to follow the military conversation, Hanyost dozed off in a chair in the corner of the small room. Some hours later, he was awakened by some rough shaking and saw Tim Murphy grinning at him. "Ready for your play-acting, you young rapscallion?"

40. Hanyost's Run
Night of August 21-22, 1777

Fortunately, Tim Murphy was just as remarkable a shooter as Benedict Arnold had said.

Binding his arms loosely with rope, Murphy and another soldier led Hanyost out of the blockhouse at dusk, putting on quite a show for the onlookers. Muttering and cursing, the rifleman pushed Hanyost roughly along.

"Here's another traitor we're not allowed to hang," Murphy complained loudly. "The blasted general says we have to turn him over to Bellinger at Fort Herkimer for more questioning. As if this scoundrel would tell us anything we'd want to know! More lies, that's all he's good for."

Marching through the fort's gate, they were soon on a narrow road along the Kuyahoora Creek. The full moon had already risen and the silvery outline of the river was visible not far ahead.

"Now, lad," whispered Murphy, slipping off the rope, and placing his double-barreled musket against his side. "Remember to do your duty at Fort Stanwix and now…run for your life!"

Needing no urging, Hanyost took off straight down the road. Two musket blasts boomed out in rapid succession, so close he could feel the blast of the balls ripping through his buckskin jacket. Behind him another shot rang out. Did they truly mean to kill him?

His chest bursting, he ran and ran, tearing through willow branches until he was knee deep in the marshes along the river. Pausing for breath, he leaned against the tangled trees and peered backward. He heard distant shouting. In the moonlight, he looked down at his buckskin jacket. Two round holes showed him how dangerously close Murphy had placed his shots.

Determined to make as much distance as he could while it was still night, Hanyost found an old Indian trail and began to jog westward. When the trail lost itself in tangled weeds, he managed to locate the road that the militia had followed not so many days past and resumed running and walking.

Exhausted and hungry by morning, he forded the river and paused to rest by the farther bank. His eyes were growing tired, and he was tempted to lie down on the soft pine needles that covered the forest floor, but the thought of his brother and the hangman's rope got him up and moving again.

Mist was rising from the river. He heard a whistle, perhaps a bird? Then again, the sound of a bird, but somehow not. Where the road turned, following the river, bushes were shaking, and there was no wind. A moment later he glimpsed Onatah's face. His friend motioned him to silence and crept closer. "Mohawk warriors are just ahead on the trail, my brother."

Hanyost stared in the direction Onatah pointed, but saw nothing in the grey dawn. "I have followed you from Fort Dayton," whispered Onatah. "Now, go and tell the story of the army of the Americans, so big it will sweep the forests into the great lake. I will circle around and come to Fort Stanwix from the other side in a few hours time."

With that, Onatah vanished back into the underbrush, so silently that Hanyost had no idea which direction he had taken. Walking along the deeply rutted road, he glimpsed dim figures in the mist before they saw him. St. Leger or Brant had sent scouts well beyond Oriskany this time. Perhaps they had already heard rumors of Arnold's force? He heard them speaking softly.

"She'kon!" he called out the Mohawk greeting. Peace!

"Hanio!" came the response. Come forward.

"I am Hanyost, brother to the Mohawk people. I have escaped from the ones who are against the King."

"Hanyost Schuyler!" Tekarihoga stepped toward him, lowering his tomahawk. Turning to his companion, the sachem said. "This is the white with the heart of a Mohawk. It is he who saved the life of Thayendenegea at Oriskany when the dog Dadawat tried to kill him."

"Come to our campfire," said the other Mohawk, grasping his hand in the Iroquois manner.

"We have heard that you were taken captive with Young Butler," said Tekarihoga.

"I was captured, this is true. But as they were taking me to put a rope around my neck and kill me, I hit the foolish soldiers and ran away. They fired their muskets but they shoot like women."

"Come with us. Thayendenegea's heart will be gladdened to see you. Already, he speaks of making the quickening ceremony for your spirit."

41. As Many as the Leaves on the Trees
August 22, 1777

When they reached the encampment of the King's native allies, Hanyost searched for the face of Ataentsic among the throng who surged toward them. He did not see her, nor did he recognize any of the warriors who crowded around, but their hostility was unmistakable. Most, by their dialects, were Cayugas or Onondagas.

Assuming that he was a prisoner, they shoved and threatened Hanyost until Tekarihoga pushed them back, shouting, "This white one is a friend of the People of the Longhouse. Do not harm him!"

Muttering, they did not move. "Stand away!" shouted Tekarihoga, brandishing his tomahawk. "We must go to Thayendenegea."

Reluctantly, the angry warriors made a space in their ranks, through which Hanyost and Tekarihoga passed. Several made chopping gestures with their tomahawks over his head but stopped short of striking.

Badly shaken, Hanyost passed many roughly constructed huts of bark-covered branches and a few tents of blankets and poles. He saw no sign of the captives. Had they all been killed? Would he be killed, too? Would all this be for nothing?

Joseph Brant was standing among a group of his closest Mohawk followers beside a bark-covered hut, too low for a man to stand within it. Smoke spiraled from a hole in the roof and a low, growling could be heard, followed by a shriek and what sounded like a flock of crows. Was this a place for torture? But no. Those sounds are not of pain, or at least not of pain alone.

Hanyost noticed that Brant's expression was one of amusement as he turned to make a whispered comment to a companion. Most of the other Indians near the small hut were Missiaugas, a primitive people whose villages lay beyond Lake Ontario. Their faces were painted completely black.

Brant's expression changed to one of undisguised joy when he recognized Hanyost. "Hanyost Schuyler, you live!" he said, embracing him. "We feared that you were dead."

The crowd around them grew larger as the Cayugas and Onondagas were joined by Old Smoke and a large crowd of Senecas. The Missiaugas looked curiously at the white man before turning their attention back to the small hut. The sounds from within now changed to a deeper and louder growling like that of a bear.

"Our friends consult the spirit of the Great Turtle," Brant smiled. "Their shaman is within the little lodge where the Turtle answers the question of whether the wild ones from beyond the great lake should stay or go, if only anyone could understand all these noises!"

The crowd around them continued to grow as more warriors from the Six Nations, and some of their women and children, drew near.

"Tell me, you who saved my life," said Brant in English, "how is it that you live and are safe among us?"

"I was captured with Young Butler," Hanyost replied in Mohawk.

"Word of this came to us." Brant switched to Mohawk. "We were told that you were both taken to the new fort near the stream Kuyahoora to be hanged."

"Yes, but the friends of Young Butler would not let him be hanged. The Big General was angry about this and said I would still be hanged. They put the rope around my neck. Here." He pointed to his neck. "My mother begged the Big General to spare my life but he is a hard man and he said I must die."

Several women in the crowd leaned forward to look at his neck, which in fact did bear scratches but only from the branches through which he had run.

"Then the soldiers took me to a place to be hanged but I had loosened the rope with which they bound my arms. When they were joking about how loudly my neck bone would crack, I ran. They fired their muskets at me."

Hanyost took off his buckskin jacket and put his fingers through the bullet holes. "See where their musket balls went."

The Indians jostled each other to get a better look at the coat. Tekarihoga took it out of Hanyost's hands and held it up over his head, calling out. "See where the foolish whites shot the coat of our friend."

"I ran and ran and they followed, shouting loudly. I hid under the reeds along the river and when they gave up their search, I came here as fast as I could."

Brant looked at the holes, and glanced skeptically at Hanyost. "These shots came pretty close," he observed in English. "It was most fortunate that you escaped in such a manner."

Hanyost could see that Brant did not fully believe him. "The Big General is coming," he said in Mohawk.

"Who do you mean by the Big General?" Brant asked, still speaking English.

Hanyost answered in Mohawk, raising his voice and adding a note of panic. "The Big General is the one called Benedict Arnold. He has brought thousands of men and hundreds of horses to Fort Dayton. He is coming here soon."

"Thousands?"

"The Big General Benedict Arnold has as many soldiers as…" he struggled for a comparison, then raised his hands to the trees overhead. "…as many as the leaves on the trees!"

The watching crowd began to murmur.

A steady chanting came from with the shaman's hut, rising and descending in volume, the animal sounds becoming more like a human language.

"As many as the leaves on the trees," Hanyost repeated. "All day and all night they marched to the fort in German Flatts and still they are coming. The army of the Big General is like…" Again he searched for an apt comparison.

The voice from within the shaman's hut grew louder and condensed into a single sound: "S'la'saat." The Missiaugas began to repeat the word over and over, picking up the rhythm of the shaman's chant. "S'la'saat! S'la'saat!"

"Like a snake," said Hanyost. "The army moves along the river from Albany like a great snake. The head of the snake comes closer to us every hour and the tail stretches over many hills and valleys behind it. Many horses beat the ground and on the first horse is the Big General with a great sword like the flame of the lightning!"

The Senecas began to understand what he was saying as one of the Mohawks who had lived among them explained Hanyost's words. "Like a snake!" cried Old Smoke. "It is as the shaman has said to the Missiauga brothers. The army is a great snake. S'la'saat is snake. The Great Turtle warns us we must flee!"

The shaman's voice grew louder and clearer, repeating other words in the Missiauga language that only a few of the Senecas could translate. "The shaman says the men of this army are like the leaves on the trees. It is a great snake coming to devour us!"

The women began to shriek and wail, demanding that their husbands leave. Several warriors were pulled from the crowd by their wives and dragged toward the huts. Other warriors laughed until their own, equally forceful Iroquois wives and mothers came and pulled them by the arm, demanding that they leave before it was too late.

As the crowd thinned out, Brant returned to English. "How fortunate that you never learned to speak Missiauga as well as Mohawk, my friend. If you had, there'd be not a man here who could withstand your unexpected eloquence."

"We will not abandon the King's men," he said in Mohawk to Tekarihoga. "Those fools will come to their senses in a little while. In the meantime, I must put more questions our friend, but in private."

"Hanyost saved your life once, Thayendenegea," said Tekarihoga. "Might not the old Tuscarora's prophecy still be true? Hanyost may be here to save your life a second time."

Brant paused. Could it be so? He looked intently at Hanyost, whose eyes were innocent of any trace of guile. "Perhaps, Tekarihoga, perhaps."

Several Tories made their way through the Indians who were now hurrying in all directions. They were startled as the naked Missiauga shaman emerged from the smoky hut, rubbing his eyes and calling out unintelligibly.

"St. Leger heard that our old friend Hanyost has come back," said Henry Nellis. "He says he wants to see him right off."

"We, too, will go to see the general," said Cornplanter, the Seneca chief, who had given up trying to dissuade his people from packing up their few belongings. "We will not go without bringing this news to the English general."

"Your white friend is the same one who brought us the warning that Herkimer was coming, is he not?" said Old Smoke, the other leader of the Senecas.

"He is," agreed Brant. "Gather your chief men, as I will mine, and we will all go to have a parley with the white general."

General Barry St. Leger, from an 18th century print

42. Moving Fast

"Walter Butler's life was spared," Hanyost was telling his story a second time to the white officers who had quickly assembled before St. Leger's tent. "Benedict Arnold decided that since Walter Butler and I were not in uniforms, we were spies, so he sentenced both of us to be hanged. Then a messenger came and he said that friends of Walter Butler had begged for his life."

"That's very likely," agreed Butler's father. "My son studied law with many young men who are now officers in the rebel army. They would not want to see him executed."

"Tell us again how you escaped," said Sir John. "It reminds me of when the angel struck off Saint Peter's chains."

"The soldiers who were guarding me thought I was a simpleton. They were making a joke about how stupid I was and did not notice that I had worked free of the rope with which they bound me."

"Hanyost does have that reputation in the valley," said Henry Nellis, "whether deserved or not. It is likely that they would think him too stupid to try to escape."

"But even if you did get your arms free, how could you have escaped from Fort Dayton?" persisted Sir John. "One of our loyal men brought us word that you and Butler were imprisoned within the fort and that they were building a gallows right there in the fort from which to hang the both of you."

St. Leger eyed him closely. "Yes, do tell us how this miraculous escape occurred. What deus ex machina intervened?

"Deus?" Hanyost stalled for time, beginning to sweat. "Benedict Arnold decided not to hang me right away. He wanted to have Peter Bellinger question me before I was hanged."

"Bellinger was at Oriskany," said Nellis, "and might be furious enough to put some pain to our friend to make him talk. Yes, I can see how Arnold might decide to hand him over to the militia. Arnold would not stoop to torture himself, but he might be willing to look the other way if someone else did his dirty work for him."

Joseph Brant was staring at Hanyost. Would he remember what Hanyost had said earlier about escaping while they were taking him to be hanged? Of course. He forgot nothing.

"Hanyost's story makes sense," said Brant, his voice steady. "There are even bullet holes in his coat."

"Putting aside for a moment the details of your marvelous escape," said St. Leger, "tell us about the size of Arnold's army."

Cornplanter said something in Seneca.

"What's that he says?" asked St. Leger.

"He says that Arnold has as many soldiers as the leaves on the trees," Brant translated.

"We go now," said Cornplanter, speaking the English words slowly and carefully. "We not die here."

He struggled for other words, then switched back to Seneca. Brant translated: " He says that too many of his people died at Oriskany. He says that you sent only Indians to die at Oriskany and kept your white soldiers safe."

"Let us not be hasty," said St. Leger. "We'll send out additional scouts to determine the location and size of this supposed relief expedition. I very much doubt that General Schuyler would detach any sizeable number of men for this purpose, not when Burgoyne's mighty force is bearing down on him."

"We cannot count on the rebel leaders acting logically," Sir John pointed out. "Remember how careless Herkimer was in marching his poor fellows right into our trap."

"In any event," said St. Leger, "we do need intelligence as to the location and disposition of Arnold's force. Once we have that, we will prepare another ambush and destroy him as thoroughly as we did Herkimer."

"Your view of the matter strikes me as very sound judgment, sir," said John Butler. "We must verify what this man Hanyost has said. My rangers can set out immediately."

"And Captain Brant, would you be willing to lead a reconnaissance in force eastward in order to locate and harry this supposed army that approaches us?"

Before Brant could answer the general, he saw several Seneca warriors, their faces painted a bright vermilion, come running from the Indian camp. "Let us see what these men can tell us. And let us hope that General Arnold is not any closer than we would desire!"

The Senecas began to speak quickly to Old Smoke and Cornplanter, while Brant struggled to translate their words as rapidly as they spilled out. "These men say that another report has come in. A Tuscarora warrior ...no, a Mohawk warrior... has just come in with the same story that Hanyost has told us. The scout says that Arnold's army is moving very quickly in this direction. He is only a few miles away. He has already passed through the valley of the dead...that is what they call Oriskany... and will be here very soon...they want Old Smoke and Cornplanter to leave immediately."

"Hold!" cried St. Leger as the Seneca chiefs stood up and turned to go. "If Arnold is truly so close, I will personally lead out a force to meet him. I will bring three hundred white men. Not all Indians. White men, too. We will fight together and defeat this rebel as we did Herkimer."

At that moment, Lieutenant Bird galloped up to the tent and leapt down from his horse. "Sir, sir," he called out in great excitement. "Two hundred of the savages have already left! They're at Wood Creek and moving fast."

"This is outrageous!" shouted St. Leger. "Shoot any man who abandons his post!"

"Begging your pardon, general," said Sir John, very calmly. "You can't shoot Indians for changing their minds in the middle of a war. It's simply their way, as my late father well knew. We can try to persuade them but we can't shoot them."

"Johnson's right," said Butler. "We cannot threaten to use force, particularly when there are so many more of them than there are of us!"

43. Brother & Sister

Hanyost joined Brant and his Mohawks as they headed back to the Indian encampment. Sir John went partway with them. The cannons continued, at regular intervals, to boom away at the fort and the few redcoats in the army manned their posts, taking occasional shots at the parapets of their enemy. The Hessians, in blue, were adjusting the firing angle of one of the Cohorn mortars.

"The Germans tried that yesterday," observed Johnson. "And I doubt if they'll have any more luck today."

"Why do you say that?" asked Brant.

"The mortars are meant to fire upward," Sir John explained. "When they are tilted forward, the powder and ball tend to tumble out."

"It's a pity," said Brant. "He'll never take the fort."

"It is my inclination to agree."

"It's a pity, too, that he would not allow us to pursue the remnants of Herkimer's forces as they fled from Oriskany."

"The British are my people, Joseph," said Sir John, "but we do have their shortcomings."

"As does every nation."

"I'll leave you here," said Johnson, shaking Brant's hand as they reached the Royal Yorkers camp. Hanyost saw that the green-coated men were clearly preparing to leave. Several had loaded their packs and others were gathering up weapons and other equipment.

"If your people depart," said Johnson, "I expect that we'll be directly behind you. But I will try to hold my men."

"As I will mine," said Brant.

When the group with Brant reached the Indian camp, they could see that panic had overtaken the Iroquois. Several Cayugas were leading away horses, loaded down with heavy bags of gunpowder.

Tekarihoga was trying to stop them. "You cannot steal the horses of the English," he was saying. When one of the Cayugas pulled a knife from his belt, Tekarihoga held up his hands. "But I am not going to kill you for the sake of an English horse."

"Where is this new scout?" asked Brant. "The one who brought the same story as Hanyost."

"He is Onatah, the brother of the healer Ataentsic. Many are listening to him now."

Turning to Hanyost, Brant looked long and hard at him. "You and Onatah were great friends as children, were you not?"

"We were," admitted Hanyost.

"Let us go and hear his words," said Brant, heading toward the large, milling circle near the huts of the Missiauga.

Hanyost saw her before he saw her brother. Ataentsic was repeating in the Missiauga language everything that her brother was saying: "The army of General Arnold is moving very fast. The men are many and they are strong. They run and do not walk toward this place. They have vowed to kill all Indian people in revenge for the killings at Oriskany."

The Missiaugas, their expressions inscrutable behind their black paint, wanted to know more.

Onatah spoke in Mohawk and again, his sister translated: "They have fast horses and will surround this place. They have great cannons, far larger than the small weak cannons of the English general. They will surround us and kill everyone."

"My sister always said that Ataentsic was very intelligent," said Brant in English. "I wonder how she learned to speak that primitive tongue so well."

"She told me that she traveled far with her sister-healers," said Hanyost. "Perhaps she spent time in the villages of those who paint their faces black."

"You were a great friend of hers, too," commented Brant, "if my recollection is correct. Molly said that you would have been happy to marry her if the trouble with that dog Dadawat had not happened."

"Perhaps."

"Perhaps, my young friend," smiled Brant, "you were never so great a fool as your fellow whites believed."

Hanyost returned his smile.

"There will be no victory here for the English, Hanyost Schuyler. But at least neither you nor I will die in this place, and that is good. Now, go welcome your friend."

Brant strode away with his Mohawks, making no effort to halt the many Indians who were streaming past him out of the camp.

Hanyost moved to the edge of the circle of Missiauga warriors. Their attention fixed on Ataentsic's every word, they did not even notice him among them.

"Now," concluded Onatah. "Go to the camp of the Cayugas. Another scout has brought word to them that the white army is only three miles away!"

As soon as Ataentsic translated Onatah's final words, the Missiaugas rushed in a great mob toward the other side of the camp, flourishing their spears and war clubs.

With their listeners suddenly gone, the brother and sister saw Hanyost.

"We have done it," said Ataentsic.

"I think we have," said Hanyost.

"We have stopped the killing," said Ataentsic.

"For now," said Hanyost, taking her hand.

44. Dusk
August 22, 1777

As dusk approached and the first few bats fluttered among the hemlocks, three people stood on a low rise above Wood Creek. The hammering of cicadas filled the air.

The three had watched as General Barry St. Leger, his bright uniform covered by a gray cape, struggled to keep his horse steady in the shallow waters of the fording place. Surrounding him, their muskets held high, his bodyguard of redcoats stayed close.

After him had come the Hessians, marching in perfect order even as the water came up to their knees and then their waists.

Sir John's men had scrambled forward across the shallow headwaters of the creek, casting anxious looks behind them. In their haste several fell and lost their muskets in the muddy stream.

Brant's mixed white and Mohawk fighters came last. They had stood at the ford since late afternoon, guarding the place where the fleeing army could have been most easily ambushed.

A cannon boomed near the fort and then another.

"St. Leger has left behind men to fire the cannons so that Gansevoort does not know that he is leaving," said Onatah.

"Perhaps the men at the cannons do not even know that he has gone."

"They will soon." Ataentsic pointed to the north where a low rise blocked their view of the fort. A large band of Missiaugas was mounting the slope, heading away from the retreat back toward the camp and the artillery emplacements.

"They go now to take what they want from the English camp."

"And those?" Hanyost pointed to several smaller bands of Indians, who had waited until the whites were across the river before spreading out and crossing over at various points above and below St. Leger's army.

"They will seek out stragglers and take their muskets. Perhaps they will take their scalps as well," said Onatah.

When the last of the English army was gone, and even the cannons fell silent, Hanyost said, "I must go back to Fort Dayton so that General Arnold will free my brother."

"I understand," said Ataentsic.

"I will go with Hanyost," said her brother. "My place is with the Oneidas and Tuscaroras who scout for the general."

"Come with us," Hanyost said to Ataentsic.

"There is no place for me there."

"But where will you go? How will I be able to find you?"

"We will find each other again, even as we did before."

45. At the Mill in Little Falls
October 18, 1777

Nicholas Schuyler stepped down from his wagon in front of the gristmill at the little falls of the Mohawk River. Tying the single weary horse to a wooden railing, he began to unload the last of the season's harvest. Flocks of Canada geese were honking overhead and a few early flakes of snow were in the wind.

The group of men who had gathered for years to gossip and exchange the latest news no longer came to the mill. Many were dead and others were with what remained of the militia at Fort Dayton. Only one other wagon stood before the mill.

Nicholas slung a heavy basket of late corn onto his shoulder and carried it into the strongly built log structure. Hannes Demuth was chatting with the miller and turned to greet him. "Looks like it'll be the last of the corn for this year."

"Yep," said Nicholas, laying down the bushel.

"No need to hurry. The pulley rope broke and Ellis's man has got to fix it before we can get our corn ground."

The miller was having some difficulty attaching a new rope to the pulley that transmitted water power to the granite grinding stones that turned the corn into flour.

"He don't want no help with it, neither," said Demuth. "May as well give you a hand with your load."

"I can manage."

"I can grab a basket or two," said Demuth. "Not doin' nothin' else for the present."

"What are you doing in these parts?" asked Nicholas as they went out to his wagon. "Your farm is out near Deerfield, ain't it?"

"It was, until the Injuns burned it. I'm staying at my cousin's place now, between here and Fort Dayton. Just helpin' out a little. He ain't got his heart in farming since his son was killed at Oriskany."

"Seems like every day I hear about somebody else who never came back."

"I was glad to learn that Hanyost didn't get himself killed, what with his not even wanting to touch a musket. I always liked the lad, no matter what they say about him."

"I heard he went off again," continued Demuth, as they carried in two more bushel baskets and emptied them next to the whirring waterwheel.

"That's true." Nicholas was not eager to talk about his brother.

The men fell silent, listening to the rushing waters of the sluiceway.

"He was a good ranger for me, I'll say that for him," said Demuth after a while. "Although I'm not sure he ever really knew what side he was on."

"That's true. He isn't really for the rebellion and he isn't a Tory, neither."

"Just wants to be let alone, I suppose. But that's hard to do in times like these."

Demuth took out his pipe, but decided against lighting it. "Wouldn't do to smoke in here. The whole place could go up in a flash."

They continued to work silently together as they waited for the miller, who was still struggling with the pulley.

"How is it workin' for George Herkimer, now that he's taken over his brother's farm?"

"Oh, not so bad," said Nicholas. "He's let the widow Mrs. Herkimer stay on in her own room."

"That's only right, Nick giving his life for his country and all."

"Of course, we're short handed since the summer."

"How's that?"

"The General took Sam and some of the best slaves with him to Oriskany and they never came back. Don't know what became of 'em."

They lapsed into silence again.

"Let's go outside where I can smoke in peace," said Demuth.

As the two men waited outside the mill, they heard hoofbeats and a moment later, Jacob Klock came galloping up.

"Here comes the new commander of our militia," said Demuth.

"Great news, boys!" he called down from his horse.

"What's the story, Jake?" asked Demuth, winking at Nicholas. "I mean, what's the report, Colonel Klock, sir?"

"Burgoyne is completely beaten!"

"Are you certain?"

"As certain as gospel," said Klock. "And Benedict Arnold is the man of the hour! Turns out he disobeyed old General Gates and went charging right into the redcoat lines. Made quite a slaughter he did, although I hear he lost his leg."

"I hope he has a better surgeon than the one who mangled Nick Herkimer's leg," offered Demuth.

"Pray God it be so," said Klock, "but there's more. A fella named Tim Murphy shot one of their big generals and after that, Burgoyne surrendered his whole army to us. Handed over his sword to General Gates."

"Who's that with you, Hannes?" Klock squinted. "Hanyost's brother, isn't it?"

Nicholas reached up to take Klock's extended hand.

"Schuyler, I've said some harsh words against your brother in the past, but I need to take them back. When he worked for me, I took him for an Injun-lovin' crazy man. He even told me I should rub bear grease on myself, like the savages do, to keep off the bugs!"

"He's always been a mite peculiar, 'tis true," said Nicholas.

"Peculiar or no, who else could have done what he did?"

"What do you mean?" asked Demuth.

"Hannes, didn't you hear how Hanyost and his Injun friend went up to Fort Stanwix and convinced the whole bunch of them devils to give up the fight?"

"I was laid up sick in the fort the day the Tories and redskins cleared out, but I always figured they was scared to face General Arnold."

"It's plain to me that Benedict Arnold would have walked into the very same trap we did, and would have gotten himself killed, except that Hanyost was clever enough to fool those superstitious heathen into running."

"Is that right?"

"Sure, this man's brother saved Arnold and Arnold saved us all at Saratoga, that's clear as day," said Klock, taking off his hat and wiping his brow.

"Who would have thought Hanyost could pull off something like that?" marveled Demuth.

"Yep, crazy Hanyost scared off St. Leger and his band of thieves and murderers, just about singlehanded, if you don't count the Injun that was with him."

Kicking his horse in the ribs, Klock soon galloped out of sight.

"You think Klock is right about all that bein' your brother's doin'?"

"I think he is, though he put my neck in the noose to do it."

"I did hear some such tale when I was at the fort, but I had that blasted camp fever and was out of my head half the time," said Demuth. "I had the idea it was him going to be hung, not you."

"It's not worth talking about."

"You don't think so?"

"I'm alive, ain't I? And so is he."

"But where's Hanyost off to now?" asked Demuth. "Has he gone back to his Tory friends?"

"Oh, he's gone west, that's all I know. Maybe Oswego or the Niagara country."

"So you're saying he's joined up with the Tories again?"

"No, that ain't it," Nicholas answered reluctantly. "It's about a woman. Some Injun girl he used to know at Connajoharry. He kept saying he wanted to go off somewhere peaceful with her."

"There ain't no place peaceful now, nor likely to be, as long as this war goes on."

"Well, I'm just telling you what he was saying."

"How'd your ma take to Hanyost going off again?" asked Demuth, as the miller finished his repairs and pulled down the great wooden lever that set the grindstones rolling.

"She told him not to fret over her," said Nicholas, shaking his head. "She said that he ought to go find that Mohawk girl."

For Further Reading

The reader is invited to explore the nineteenth century histories, which are the source of this tale. Excerpts from several can be found at the end of this book.

These sources, which I closely followed as to the sequence of events in the book, are readily found on the Internet.

The authors, who had often interviewed elderly survivors of the Revolution, include:

Nathaniel S. Benton, *History of Herkimer County* (1854)

William W. Campbell, *Annals of Tryon County; or, the Border Warfare of New York, During the Revolution* (1831)

William Leete Stone, *Life of Joseph Brant* (1838)

Harold Frederic, *The Mohawk Valley During the Revolution* (1877)

For those interested in primary sources, I recommend reading the very detailed records kept by Nicholas Herkimer and his associates from 1775 to 1783 in *The Minute Book of The Committee of Safety of Tryon County*, available on the Internet. Also of interest is Nicholas Schuyler's 1829 petition for a pension based on a claim of military service during the Revolution, which includes his version of his brother's role in the great events of 1777. James Morrison deserves much credit for his work in preserving and making available to the public this and numerous other Revolutionary War pension documents. (http:// morrisonspensions.org)

It should be noted that during the period of this story, Fort Stanwix was briefly known as Fort Schuyler, but the name caused confusion due to the existence of several other Fort Schuylers in New York State at the same time. To avoid this confusion, I have consistently used the term Fort Stanwix in this book. William Colbrath's personal record of life inside the fort was a valuable source for this novel, and has been reprinted as *Days of Siege; A Journal of the Siege of Fort Stanwix in 1777* (Eastern National books, 1983)

The National Monument of Fort Stanwix in Rome, NY includes the Marinus Willett Education Center and a very accurate reconstruction of the 1777 fort. General Herkimer's original home near Little Falls is preserved as a New York State Historical Site and both sites are well worth visiting by those interested in this crucial era in American history

Throughout the book I use the spelling "Connajoharry" for the Mohawk village that stood on the south bank of the Mohawk River between Little Falls and Fort Plain, NY. I use this spelling to avoid confusion with the village of Canajoharie which is several miles further east. The Anglican chapel built by Sir William Johnson, and known for many years as Indian Castle Church, is all that remains of the Mohawk village.

An important point in terms of nomenclature is that the Six Nations refer to themselves as the "Haudensaunee," which translates to "The People of the Longhouse." In this book I use the more common term "Iroquois." The Mohawks call themselves "Kanienkehaka," which has been translated as People of the Flint.

There are a number of fine modern histories of the Revolution in the Mohawk Valley which include:

Barbara Graymont, *The Iroquois in the American Revolution* (1972)

Isabel Thompson Kelsay, *Joseph Brant 1743-1807, Man of Two Worlds* (1984)

Fintan O'Toole, *White Savage: William Johnson and the Invention of America* (2005)

Joseph T. Glatthaar and James Kirby Martin, *Forgotten Allies, The Oneida Indians and the American Revolution* (2006)

Alan Taylor, *The Divided Ground; Indians, Settlers and the Northern Borderland of the American Revolution,* (2006)

Last but certainly not least, I recommend Walter Edmonds' very vivid novel of the same time and place, *Drums Along the Mohawk* (1936) which is now back in print thanks to Syracuse University Press. I must echo his words in that I, too, was "astonished to see how a simple narration of the experiences of these actual people carried the book along with only slight liberties with truth." Very few of the people in the book have been imagined, as can be seen from the list of characters, which follows.

Characters

Only those designated (*) are fictional.

Family

Hanyost Schuyler
Nicholas Schuyler, his brother
Elizabeth Barbara Schuyler, his mother
Peter Schuyler, his father (d. 1765)
Johan Herkimer, his uncle, sided with Loyalists in
the American Revolution
Nicholas Herkimer, his uncle, commander of the
Tryon County militia

The Mohawks

"Black Jacob"* a Tuscarora wanderer who
befriends the young Hanyost
Joseph Brant, protégé of Sir William Johnson and
leader of Mohawks opposing the Revolution
Molly Brant, his sister and wife of Sir William
Johnson
Onatah * friend of Hanyost
Ataentsic* sister of Onatah
Dadawat* an older Mohawk boy
Tekarihoga, titular chief of the Mohawks

Supporters of Independence

Benedict Arnold, regarded as the hero of Saratoga, but later reviled as a traitor

Colonel Peter Bellinger of the Tryon County Militia, married to Hanyost's Aunt Delia

Lieutenant Colonel Frederick Bellinger, captured at Oriskany

Hannes Demuth, captain in the Tyron County Militia

Andrew Fink, member of the Tryon County Committee of Public Safety

Major John Frey, captured at Oriskany

Colonel Peter Gansevoort, commander at Fort Stanwix

Jacob Gardinier, known for his heroism at Oriskany

Adam Helmer, Herkimer's messenger, later carried warning to settlers of Tory raiders

Abel Hunt, killed at Oriskany

George Klock, persistent claimant for Indian lands

Jacob Klock, commander of the Tryon County militia after Oriskany

Tim Murphy, known as a rifleman and credited by some for the victory at Saratoga

John Schults, fought at Oriskany and survived

Jim Seeber, killed at Oriskany

Rudolph Seeber, killed at Oriskany

General Philip Schuyler, commander of American forces in New York, replaced just before battle of Saratoga by General Gates

Thomas Spencer, Oneida scout, killed at Oriskany

George Van Deusen, fought at Oriskany and survived

Colonel Frederick Vischer, blamed for fleeing from Oriskany

Edward Wall, member of the Tryon County

Committee of Public Safety
Colonel Weston, commander at Fort Dayton
Colonel Marinus Willett, known for many exploits
    during the Revolution
Richard Woolover, listed as killed at Oriskany

Loyalists and British

Sir William Johnson (d. 1774) Indian
    Superintendent for the Crown
Sir John Johnson, his son
Guy Johnson, his nephew
John Butler, his agent and later leader of Loyalist
    rangers
Walter Butler, his son
Alec MacGregor* a Scot slain at Oriskany
Henry Nellis, onetime friend of George Klock
Peter Tenbrook, reported to have deserted from
    militia with Johan Herkimer
Old Smoke, Seneca leader at Fort Stanwix
Cornplanter, Seneca leader at Fort Stanwix
General Barry St. Leger, commander of the
    expedition against Fort Stanwix
Lieutenant Bird, his aide
General John Burgoyne, commander of the major
    British offensive in 1777, defeated at Saratoga

Excerpts from selected 19th century sources

History of Herkimer County Nathaniel S. Benton (1854)

Annals of Tryon County; or, the Border Warfare of New York, During the Revolution by William W. Campbell (1831)

Petition of Nicholas Schuyler claiming a pension for services in the Revolution from Chapter Five, *History of Herkimer County* by Nathaniel S. Benton (1854)

General Arnold arrived at Fort Dayton a short time before the 21st of August, at which point troops were assembling with a view of proceeding to the relief of Fort (Stanwix), still beleaguered by St. Leger's forces, and to counteract the effect of the incendiary efforts of Johnson, Claus and John Butler. The American general on the 20th of August, issued a proclamation stating that "whereas a certain Barry St. Leger, a Brigadier-General in the service of George of Great Britain, at the head of a banditti of robbers, murderers and traitors, composed of savages of America and more savage Britons (among whom is the noted Sir John Johnson, John Butler and Daniel Claus), have lately appeared in the frontiers of this state, and threatened ruin and destruction to all the inhabitants of the United States, urging the inhabitants to continue their fidelity to the common cause, offering pardon to all those who may have been misled by the artifice and misrepresentation of the enemy, if they would in ten days come in and lay down their arms, but announcing the just vengeance of heaven and of this exasperated country against all who should persist in their wicked courses." On the 23d of August Gen. Arnold left Fort Dayton, determined to hazard a battle with forces inferior to the enemy before Fort (Stanwix), rather than have the garrison surrender, and had proceeded half a day's march, when he was met by an express from Col. Gansevoort, with cheering news that the siege had been raised; but the cause of this sudden movement on the part of the enemy was wholly unknown to the gallant Colonel and his brave garrison; not so however with Arnold.

Hanyost Schuyler was the instrument made use of to scatter the besieging forces surrounding Fort (Stanwix), and send them helter-skelter back to Canada in double quick time. The home of this strange and singular being, was near the upper Mohawk Indian castle in the present town of Danube, where he resided with his mother and brother Nicholas, and hence in early life had much intercourse with the Indians. He is described as coarse and ignorant, and but little removed from idiocy, and still possessing shrewdness enough to be made the instrument of accomplishing an important object. Hanyost was somewhat tainted with loyalty, and had been captured at Shoemaker's with Walter N. Butler, and others. He was tried by a court martial and sentenced to death. His mother and brother, on hearing this sad news, of course hastened to headquarters to intercede for his life. For a time their efforts were unavailing, but finally it was proposed he should repair to St. Leger's camp with a friendly Oneida Indian, and so manage to alarm the enemy as to produce an abandonment of the siege.

Hanyost gladly embraced the alternative, leaving his brother as a hostage for the faithful execution of his mission; being assured that Nicholas should die if he faltered in the enterprise. Schuyler having procured sundry shots through his garments, that he might show he had run for dear life, departed with his Indian comrade for the enemy's camp. They had arranged between them to approach St. Leger's position from opposite directions, and were not to appear acquainted with each other, if they should meet. This affair was wisely planned, and most skillfully and adroitly executed. The instrument was well chosen. He was well known as a loyalist, and the parties to whom he first addressed himself were no unwilling auditors, nor in an unfavorable mood to be deeply impressed and even awed by his ambiguous language and mysterious manner. The native American Indians, like the followers of Mahomet, were ever inspired with a peculiar respect and even reverence for idiots and lunatics. Fraternal regard strongly prompted Hanyost to apply all his energies and to leave no effort untried to secure the complete success of his mission, and relieve his brother

271

from the fate that was hanging over him. He was completely successful, and having followed the retreating enemy to Wood Creek, he there left them, and returned to Fort (Stanwix) the same evening, and gave Col. Gansevoort the first intimation of Arnold's approach. It was not until Schuyler's arrival at the fort, that its commandant was able to solve the problem of St. Leger's sudden departure and precipitate flight.

Hanyost returned to the German Flats where his brother was released from confinement, to the great gratification of his mother and relatives, but he was too strongly imbued with sentiments of loyalism, to resist giving a permanent adherence to the interests of the crown, and in the fall of the same year went to Canada and remained there until the close of the war, when he returned to the Mohawk valley, where he died about forty-five years since.

The project of sending Schuyler in advance to announce Gen. Arnold's approach to the besieging forces, has been attributed to that officer. Such an idea however is not characteristic of the man. The forces on the march were not equal to the enemy then before Fort (Stanwix), in point of numbers, but they were chiefly composed of continental light troops, endured to service and accustomed to obey, and the patriotic militia of the country had again rallied to the defense of their homes and families, eager for the strife and determined on revenge. Under such circumstances, knowing the strength of the garrison, and being, without doubt, well advised of the position and numbers of the enemy, the American forces all told were a match for their opponents in the neighborhood of the fort, and it was by no means likely St. Leger would again attempt to interrupt the approach of the provincials by offering battle on any other field, and by dividing his strength hazard the safety of the camp in another sortie.

Reflections somewhat like these would be presented to the mind of the American commander, who was brave and intemperately rash, and who would delight in scourging the men he had denounced as a "banditti of robbers, murderers and traitors," and therefore would be less likely to suggest a stratagem to avoid a battle than some one possessing a different temperament. The probability is that this project did not originate with Arnold, although on reflection, while impatiently waiting at Fort Dayton for reinforcements and supplies, he acquiesced in the measure, at the same time, perhaps, doubting its success.

from *Annals of Tryon County; or, the Border Warfare of New York, During the Revolution* by William W. Campbell (1831)

From this place, a few days before, Gen. Arnold sent forward Hanyost Schuyler, a refugee, to the camp of St. Leger. He had given him his liberty, on condition that he would announce his approach, and make an exaggerated statement of his forces. He retained his brother as an hostage.

In the camp of St. Leger all was confusion. The Indians, disappointed in obtaining plunder, and enraged on account of their losses, could scarcely be restrained. They supposed that in the action they had fired across and killed each other. The confusion was greatly increased by the arrival of Schuyler. On being questioned as to the number of troops approaching, he answered that he knew not, but they were as numerous as the leaves upon the forest trees. The Indians refused to remain any longer. All the arts of their leaders were unavailing. On the 22d of August, St. Leger retired in great confusion, leaving the camp with a great part of his baggage. The Indians plundered from their friends in the retreat, and it is said raised a shout, that the Americans were coming, and then amused themselves in witnessing the terror it occasioned. St. Leger has been accused by his subaltern officers of a want of energy. He is said to have been in a state of intoxication, during most of the time his forces lay before the fort.

Thus ended the siege of Fort (Stanwix), and a campaign, which, at the commencement, threatened the valley of the Mohawk with conquest and devastation.

from the Petition of Nicholas Schuyler claiming a pension for services in the Revolution (1827)

Copy from the National Archives
Record of the U. S. House of Representatives
Record Group 233
Congress 21st Committee on Military Pensions
File Number HR 21AD16.1
Transcribed E. R. Hessler 2/87

To the Congress of the United States

The Petition of Nicholas Schuyler of the Town of Danube in the County of Herkimer and State of New York Respectfully Sheweth

That your Petitioner has during the Revolutionary War rendered important service in defence of his country and that although not enlisted into the regular service of the country yet in the New York State Militia and by other Service has contributed, as he hopes, very essentially to the achievement of that Independence which is at this time the pride and the glory as well as the peculiar blessing of the American People.

That your Petitioner on one particular occasion during said war by a voluntary pledge of his life for the performance of a high and dangerous trust has as your Petitioner flatters himself under divine providence been the happy means to save from certain and otherwise inevitable massacre about six hundred of the Patriots of the Revolution.

The instance to which your Petitioner refers is the investment of Fort Schuyler (commonly called Fort Stanwix) by a numerous party of Indians and Tories commanded by Col. St. Leger in the year 1777 and where, but for the timely service of your Petitioner Col. Gansevoort and Willett with the garrison consisting of about six hundred men being already reduced to the utmost extremity would inevitably have fallen victims to savage barbarity.

The manner in which their deliverance was effected is the following:

Honyost Schuyler the Brother of your Petitioner had shortly after the commencement of the Revolution enlisted into the regular service of the United States, from which after a short term of service he deserted and went to Canada where he enlisted into the British Service, and came with the army of Col. St. Leger to the siege of Fort Schuyler. From Fort Schuyler the said Honyost accompanied by a number of the enemy and among them Walter Butler (or young Butler as he was generally called) who was distinguished for the many and frequent depravations and murders which he caused to be committed upon our border settlements upon the Mohawk, came to Herkimer under the pretense of having been sent as a flag of truce from Col. St. Leger, whereby the order of General Benedict Arnold who with several regiments of continental troops was at that time stationed at Fort Dayton (now Herkimer) they were all seized as spies and tried by a Court Martial and the said Han Yost having been found guilty of desertion was sentenced to be shot; that when the sentence was made known to your Petitioner, your Petitioner and his then aged Mother immediately repaired to the quarters of General Arnold to intercede with the general in behalf of the said Honyost and to implore a pardon for him; that as to the petitions & entreaties of your Petitioner and his Mother General Arnold for a long time remained inflexible, until finally, being aware of the critical situation of our garrison at Fort Schuyler & the extreme danger of its falling into the hands of an infuriated and savage enemy and that the said Honyost Schuyler from his known confidence among that enemy might be serviceably employed in the relief of that garrison, the General made to your Petitioner the following proposition:

That a pardon should be granted to the said Honyost on the condition that the said Honyost would immediately and with the utmost expedition proceed to Fort Schuyler and there by a misrepresentation of the strength and movement of General Arnold's army induce the enemy to abandon the siege of that fort and would then return to General Arnold and surrender himself up; and on the further condition that your Petitioner would in the meantime submit himself to imprisonment in the room of his brother the said Honyost; and would also agree to a forfeiture of his your Petitioners life, and would consent to be executed in the stead of the said Honyost in case the said Honyost should not again return;

That your Petitioner after a consultation with his Brother the said Honyost upon the subject of the proposal acceded to the proposition aforesaid made to him your Petitioner by General Arnold; That your Petitioner was actually imprisoned at Fort Dayton in the room of the said Honyost during the absence of the said Honyost to Fort Schuyler and had positively pledged the forfeiture of his life and did expect to be and does now believe that the your Petitioner would have been executed in the event that the said Honyost had failed in the performance of his trust; That the said Honyost upon the imprisonment of your Petitioner in his stead was set at liberty and did immediately proceed to Fort Schuyler and there by exaggerating the force of General Arnold and representing him and his army as rapidly advancing towards the enemy, produced such panic and consternations among our savages, the enemy as caused them, against the protestations and effort of Col. St. Leger, to hasten their departure from the Fort with the utmost precipitation and so completely panic struck were the enemy that by the report brought to them by the said Honyost that they fled to their boats and pushed off leaving behind them their tents, and baggage and other camp equipage which fell into hands of our garrison. Col. Gansevoort and his veterans were thereby relieved and immediately after abandoned the Fort and thus happily escaped that butchery which otherwise was to have been their inevitable destiny. The said Honyost after proceeding with the enemy down Wood Creek for some distance effected his escape and returned to our garrison in the Fort and shortly thereafter came to Herkimer to General Arnold by whose order he received his pardon and your Petitioner his release from imprisonment...

Your Petitioner would therefore pray your honorable body to provide out of the funds of the general government, in considerations of the suffering and service of your Petitioner his present destitute condition a pension or yearly allowance in money such as may be adequate to the want and condition of your aged Petitioner, as will procure for him and his family during the few remaining days of his life the necessary comforts of old age; and as under all the circumstances shall by your honorable body be deemed reasonable and right.

And as in duty bound your Petitioner will ever pray.*

Oct. 17, 1827 (Signed) Nicholas Schuyler

*His petition for a pension was rejected.

The author was born in Little Falls near the scenes of this story. He first heard the tale of Hanyost from his father Edward Cooney, a local historian and a founder of the Little Falls Historical Society. After working for thirty-five years as an English teacher and school administrator in the New York City public schools, Michael Cooney is currently employed as a curriculum specialist for Teachers College, Columbia University.

He and his wife Barbara are the parents of three daughters and have five grandchildren.

www.ingramcontent.com/pod-product-compliance
Lightning Source LLC
Chambersburg PA
CBHW060342030726
47497CB00003B/571